KELLIE HAILES declared at the age of five that she was going to write books when she grew up. It took a while for her to get there, with a career as a radio copywriter, freelance copywriter and web writer filling the dream-hole, until now. Kellie lives on an island-that's-not-really-an-island in New Zealand with her patient husband, funny little human and neurotic cat. When the characters in her head aren't dictating their story to her, she can be found taking short walks, eating good cheese and jonesing for her next coffee fix.

**Also by
Kellie Hailes**

The Big Little Festival
Christmas at the Second Chance Chocolate Shop
The Little Unicorn Gift Shop

The Cosy Coffee Shop of Promises

Kellie Hailes

ONE PLACE. MANY STORIES

HQ
An imprint of HarperCollins*Publishers* Ltd
1 London Bridge Street
London SE1 9GF

This edition 2019

1
First published in Great Britain by
HQ, an imprint of HarperCollins*Publishers* Ltd 2017

Kellie Hailes asserts the moral right to be
identified as the author of this work.
A catalogue record for this book is
available from the British Library.

ISBN 978-0-00-835228-8

MIX
Paper from
responsible sources
FSC™ C007454

This book is produced from independently certified FSC™ paper
to ensure responsible forest management.

For more information visit: www.harpercollins.co.uk/green

This book is set in 11/16 pt. Sabon

Printed and bound in Great Britain by
CPI Group (UK) Ltd, Croydon, CR0 4YY

For Aaron, who always believed in me.

CHAPTER ONE

'Wine. Now. And don't get mouthy with me.'

Mel watched Tony's sea-blue eyes light up as his lips parted slightly...

'What's got your knick...'

'I'm serious,' she cut in, before he had a chance to be the second person to grind her gears that day. 'I'm in no mood for your cheek. And I can tell by that twitchy jaw of yours that you're contemplating still trying to give me some.' Mel took off her navy peacoat and shuddered as wintry air wrapped its way around her thin form. She promptly buttoned up again and tugged her scarf tighter around her neck. 'All I want from you is for you to do your job, pour me a glass of Pinot Gris and leave me to drink it, alone, and in peace. And why is it so cold in here? It's freezing out. It shouldn't be freezing in.' She shook her head. 'No matter. I don't care. The wine will warm me up.'

'Bu...'

'No. No buts. No whys. No questions.' She pointed to

I

the glass-doored fridge. 'Just get the bottle, get a glass, and pour.' Mel gave Tony her best glare, hoping to get past his notoriously thick skin.

She watched the muscles in his jaw continue to work, as if debating whether to ignore her order to be left in peace or do that clichéd 'had a bad day, tell me about it' barman patter. Sensibility must have won, because he turned and bent over to grab a bottle of Pinot Gris from the chiller, giving her a fantastic view of his toned and rounded rear. A view she'd usually take a moment to appreciate, but not right now, not after the unexpected, and not in a good way, phone call she'd just received from her mother.

Tony sloshed the wine into a tired-looking, age-speckled glass, pushed it in her direction, then punched at the card machine. 'Here you go,' he said, proffering the handset.

Mel squinted at the numbers on the screen. 'Tony, um, that's not right. You've overcharged me.'

'No, that's the price.' Tony nodded, but kept his eyes firmly on the bar. 'Since the beginning of this week.'

'Really? You can't tell me a bottle of wine rose in price by almost double in the space of seven days?'

'You're right, it hasn't.' He glanced up. 'But the hole in my muffler is yelling at me to put the prices up. And I haven't in years, so...'

'Oh. Okay. Sorry.' Mel handed over her bank card, embarrassed to have questioned the price rise. She'd heard the village gossip. Tony's business wasn't doing so well. Apparently hadn't been for years, but had got worse since his dad passed away the year before. Not that she knew much about that. She'd been new to town, and didn't want to get a reputation as a gossip, so had only heard the odd conversation here and there over the coffee cups in her café, nothing more.

'So, are you going to just stare into that glass of wine or are you going to drink it? Because I don't have a funnel to pour it back into the bottle. Although reselling it would make my mechanic happier faster. And if you buy two glasses I might even be able to afford to put the heating on.'

Mel shot Tony a grateful smile. Despite his infamous reputation as a ladies' man, he was also known about the small farming town of Rabbits Leap as being something of a gentleman and had quite the knack of making you feel at ease, which, considering her current heightened state of irritation, was quite a feat.

'You're still not taking a sip, or a slug. And, well, it sounds like you needed a slug.'

Mel narrowed her eyes at Tony, hoping to scare him into shutting up with a stern look. 'What did I say about getting mouthy? And teasing for that matter?'

'I'm not teasing. You look pale. Paler than usual, and you know you're pretty pale, so you're almost translucent right now. Even the bright streaks of pink in your hair are looking a little less hot.'

'You pay attention to my hair colour?' Mel's hand unconsciously went to her hair and tucked a stray lock behind her ears. Tony looked at her hair? Since when? She'd always assumed he'd seen her as nothing more than a regular customer, a friendly acquaintance, not someone to take notice of. Sure, they got along well enough, would chat for a moment or two if they passed each other on the street, or if it was quiet in the pub, but that was the extent of their relationship.

'Well, you're about the most exciting thing to happen in this place for the last ten years…'

'Me? Exciting?' A tingle of pleasure stirred within her.

Tony winked and turned that tingle into a zing. Since her last boyfriend, the local vet, had taken off to care for animals overseas, Mel hadn't had any action, let alone a compliment, from a man. And apparently, if that unexpected zing frenzy that had zipped through her body was anything to go by, she'd been craving it.

'Yeah, exciting.' Tony's glance lingered on her face, as if drinking her in. 'And pretty, too.'

She rolled her eyes, trying to ignore the way her body reacted to the words of approval. She picked up her glass and took the suggested slug. She was being stupid. Tony wasn't calling *her* exciting, just her hair. And the only reason he was calling her pretty was because that's what he did; he called women pretty, he charmed them, he took them to bed, and that was that. And she'd had enough of her love life – heck, her life in general – ending with 'that was that' to be interested in someone who'd pretty much created the phrase.

'Feel better?' His eyes, usually dancing with humour, were crinkled at the corners with concern.

'Not really.'

'Have another slug.'

As she lifted the glass she glanced around the bar, taking in the bar leaners with their tired, ring-stained, laminated tops and obsolete ashtrays in their centres. The tall stools next to them looked rickety from decades of propping up farmers, the pool table needed a resurface, and as for the dartboard… it was covered in so many tiny pin holes it was amazing a dart could stay wedged in it. The village chatter was right, Tony was having a tough time…

Her eyes fell on a machine sitting at the far end of the bar. All shiny and silvery and gleaming with newness. That shouldn't be there.

Her blood heated up, and not in an 'oh swoon, a man just complimented me' kind of way.

'What is that?' Mel seethed through gritted teeth.

She couldn't believe what she was seeing. What was he thinking? Did he have it in for her, too? Was it 'Let's Piss Off Mel Day'? She'd moved to Rabbits Leap just over a year ago to try and create a sense of security for herself. A place she could settle down in, call home, maybe even meet a nice, normal guy she could fall in love with. And in one day what little security she'd carefully built was in danger of being blown apart. First her mother calling to tell her she was coming to town and bringing her special brand of crazy with her, and now this?

'What's what?' The crinkles of concern further deepened.

'That.' She pointed to the cause of her ire.

'The coffee machine?'

'Yeah, the coffee machine. The coffee machine that should not be in your bar, because I have a coffee machine. In my café. The only café in the village. You remember that? The one place a person can get a good cup of coffee? The place that just happens to be my livelihood, and you want to screw with it?'

Tony took a step back as if he'd been hit with a barrage of arrows. *Good.* His eyebrows gathered in a frown. But he didn't look sorry. Why didn't he look sorry? And why had he straightened up and stopped looking stricken?

'It's just business, Mel.'

'And it's just a small village, Tony.'

She looked at her wine and considered throwing the contents of it over him, then remembered how much it had cost. Taking the glass, she brought it to her mouth and tipped it back, swallowing the lot in one long gulp.

She set the glass back on the bar, gently, so he wouldn't see how shaken she was. 'There's only enough room in this village for one coffee machine.' She mentally slapped herself as the words came out with a wobble, not as the threat she'd intended.

'And what does that mean?' Tony folded his arms and leant in towards her, his eyebrow raised.

Mel gulped. He wanted her to throw down the gauntlet? Fine then. 'It means you can try to make coffee. You can spend hours trying to get it right, make thousands of cups, whatever. But your coffee will never be as good as mine and all you'll have is a big hunk of expensive metal sitting unloved at the end of your bar.'

'Sounds like you're challenging me to a coffee-off.'

How could Tony be so cavalier? So unfazed by the truth? He'd spent a ton of money on something he'd only end up regretting.

Mel took a deep breath, picked up her wallet and walked to the door. She spun round to face her adversary.

'There's no challenge here. All you're good for is pulling a pint or three. Coffee? That's for the adults. You leave coffee to me.'

She leant into the old pub door, pushed it with all her might and lurched over the threshold into the watery, late-winter sun and shivered. Could today get any worse?

***

7

Had he done the wrong thing? Was buying that ridiculous monstrosity and installing it in the pub a stupid idea? He'd spent the last decent chunk of money he had to get it. What if it didn't fly? What would happen next? He couldn't keep the place open on the smell of a beer-soaked carpet, but he couldn't fail either. It was all he had left to remind him of his family. The Bullion had been his dad's baby. The one thing that had kept his dad sane after his mother had passed away. More than that, it was where what few solid memories he had of his mother were. Her smiling at him as he sat at the kitchen table munching on a biscuit while she cooked in the pub's kitchen. The violet scent of her perfume as she'd pulled his four-year-old self into a cuddle after he'd fallen from a bar stool while on an ambitious mountaineering expedition.

Then there was the promise he'd made to his father, the final words they'd shared as his father breathed his last. His vow to preserve The Bullion's history, to keep her alive. Dread tugged at his heart. What if he couldn't keep that promise?

God, why couldn't his father have been more open, more honest with him about their financial situation? Why couldn't he have put away his pride for one second and seen a bank manager, cap in hand, asked for a… Tony shoved the idea away. No. That wasn't an option. Not then. Not now. The McArthurs don't ask for help. That was his dad's number-one rule. A rule his father had also drilled into him. No, he wasn't going cap in hand to a bank manager. He didn't even own a cap, anyway. He just had to come up with some new ideas to breathe life into the old girl. The coffee machine had been one of them, and he'd spent the last of his personal savings buying it.

But what if Mel was right? What if he couldn't make a good coffee? Heck, what if she stole into the pub in the middle of the night and tampered with it so he couldn't?

Tony shook his head. The potential for poverty was turning him paranoid. Besides, the coffee machine was a great idea. Lorry drivers were always stopping in looking for a late-night cup, and who knew? Maybe the locals would like a cup of herbal tea or something before heading home after a big night.

Buy herbal tea. He added the item to his mental grocery list, along with bread, bananas and milk. Maybe he'd see if there was any of that new-age herbal tea stuff that made you sleep. Normally he'd do what his dad had always done and have a cup of hot milk with a dash of malt to send him off. But lately it hadn't done the trick and he'd spent more hours tossing and turning than he had actually sleeping, his mind ticking over with mounting bills, mounting problems and not a hell of a lot of solutions. Heck, he was so bone-tired he wasn't even all that interested in girls. Maybe that was the problem? Maybe he needed to tire himself out...

'Hey, baby brother!'

'Might be. But I'm still taller than you.' Tony grinned at his sister and two nephews as they piled into the pub. 'How you doing, you little scallywags?'

'Scallywags?!'

Tony laughed as the boys feigned insult and horror in perfect unison.

'You heard me. Now come and give your old uncle a hug.'

The boys flew at him, nearly knocking him over as they hurled themselves into his outstretched arms. He drew them in and held them, breathing in the heady mix of mud and cinnamon scent that he was pretty sure they'd been born with.

'Have we cuddled you long enough? Can we have a lemonade now?' Tyler peered up at him with a hopeful eye.

'And a bag of crisps?' asked Jordan, his voice filled with anticipation, and just a hint of cheek.

'Each?' They pleaded in perfect unison.

Two peas in a pod those boys were. And the loves of Jody's life. Since the day she'd found out she'd fallen pregnant to a man she'd met during a shift at the pub, a random, a one-nighter, she'd sworn off all men until the boys were old enough to fend for themselves.

Tony watched as the boys grabbed a bag of crisps each and poured two glasses of lemonade and wondered at what point Jody would decide they were old enough, because at nine they looked pretty well sorted, and he was pretty sure he spotted flashes of loneliness in her eyes when she saw couples holding hands over the bar's leaners.

'So what's with the shiny new toy?' Jody jerked her head down towards the end of the bar.

'It's what's going to save this place.'

Jody snorted and took a sip of Tyler's lemonade, ignoring his wail of displeasure. 'It's going to take a whole lot more than coffee to save this dump.'

Tony bristled. Just because this place wasn't the love of her life it didn't mean it wasn't the love of his, and just as she wouldn't hear a bad word said about her boys, he didn't like a bad word said...

'And don't get all grumpy on me, Tony McArthur. I know you love this joint, but it needs more than one person running it. You need to...'

'If you say settle down, I'll turn the soda dispenser on you.'

'Oooh, soda water, colour me scared.'

'Not soda, dear sister. Raspberry fizzy. Sweet, sticky and staining.'

Jody stuck her tongue out. 'But you should, you know, settle down. It'll do you good having a partner in crime.'

'You're one to talk.'

'I'm well settled down and I've got two partners in crime, right, boys?'

Tony laughed again as the boys rolled their eyes, then took off upstairs to his quarters where his old gaming console lay gathering dust.

'Besides, you're only going to piss off the café girl with that machine in here. You're treading on her turf, and frankly it's not a particularly gentlemanly thing to do.'

Heat washed over Tony's face. Even though he had a reputation for liking the ladies, he always tried to treat them well. But that was pleasure, and this was business. Not just business, it was life and death. Actually, it was livelihood or death. And he intended to keep on kicking for as long as possible. Without the bar he was nothing. No one.

'Well, I can see by the flaming shame on your face that she's seen it.'

'Yep,' he sighed. The more he looked at the hunk of metal the worse he felt about what he'd done. There was an unspoken rule among the business people of Rabbits Leap that they didn't poach customers. It was akin to stealing. Yet he'd done just that in a bid to save The Bullion. What was worse, he'd done it to a member of the community he actually respected and always had time for.

'Tony, you've got to apologise, and then take the machine back. Do something. It's a small town and the last thing you need is to be bad-mouthed or to lose customers. Find a way to make it work.'

***

Ting-a-ling.

Mel looked up from arranging a fresh batch of scones on a rose-printed vintage cake stand to see who'd walked in, her customer-ready smile fading as she saw her tall, broad-shouldered, blond, wavy-haired nemesis.

'Get out.' Her words were cool and calm, the opposite of the fire burning in her veins, in her heart. No one was taking away her café, her chance at a stable life, especially not a pretty boy who was used to getting what he wanted with a smile and a wink.

'Is that any way to treat a customer?'

'You're not a customer. You never have been. I've not seen you step foot in here since I opened up – not once.' Mel pointed to the door. 'So get out.'

'Well, maybe it's time I decided to change that. And besides…'

She watched Tony take in the quiet café. Empty, bar her two regulars, Mr Muir and Mrs Wellbelove, who were enjoying their cups of tea and crosswords in separate silence.

'…It looks like you need the business.'

Mel rankled at the words as they hit home. She'd hoped setting up in Rabbits Leap would be a good, solid investment, that it would give her security. But that 'security' was looking as tenuous as her bank balance. The locals weren't joking when they said it was 'the town that tourism forgot'. In summer the odd tourist ambled through, lost, on their way to Torquay. But, on seeing there was nothing more than farms and hills, they quickly ambled out again. As for winter? You could've lain down all day in the middle of the street without threat of being run over. And this winter had been worse, what with farmers shutting up shop due to milk prices falling even further.

'Really? I need the business?' She raised an eyebrow, hoping the small act of defiance would annoy him as much as he'd annoyed her. 'I'm not the one putting prices up. Unlike someone else standing before me...'

Tony threw his hands up in the air as if warding the words off.

Good, she'd got to him.

'Look, Mel, I'm not here to fight.'

'Then what are you here for?'

'Coffee. A flat white. And a scone. They look good.'

'They are good.'

'Then I'll take one.' Tony rubbed his chin. 'Actually, make that two.'

Mel faked ringing up the purchase on the vintage cash register she'd found after scouring auction sites for weeks and weeks. 'That'll be on the house.'

'That's a bit cheap, isn't it?' Tony's lips lifted in a half-smile.

'It's on me. A man desperate enough to install a coffee machine in a pub clearly needs a bit of charity.' Yes, Tony was trying to take business away from her, but really, how much of a threat would he be to her business anyway? It wasn't like he could actually make a decent cup of coffee.

'So, are you going to stand there staring at me like I'm God's gift or are you going to give me my free scones?'

Mel blushed.

'Sorry, I wasn't staring. Just…'

'Imagining me kissing you. Yeah, yeah, I know. Don't worry, you're not the first woman.'

'I wasn't.' Mel sputtered, horrified. 'I wouldn't.'

'I know. I'm teasing. Relax.'

The word had the opposite effect. Mel's body coiled up, ready to attack at the next thing he said that irritated her.

Why was he having this effect on her? Usually nothing ruffled her feathers, or her multicoloured hair. She'd weathered so much change in her life that something as small as someone making an attempt to kill off her coffee business should be laughable. But as she looked into his handsome and openly amused face she wanted to take up her tongs, grab his earlobe in its metal claws, give it a good twist, then drag him to the door and shove him out of it. Instead, she picked up the tongs, fished two scones out onto a plate, added a pat of butter and passed the plate to him.

'Can you just… sit. I'll bring your coffee to you.'

With a wink and a grin Tony did exactly as she asked, leaving her to make his coffee in peace. The familiar ritual of grinding the beans, tamping them down, smelling the rich aroma of the coffee as it dripped into a cup while she heated the milk relaxed her, so much more than a man telling her to relax ever would. Maybe the problem wasn't that he was trying to ruin her business; maybe it was that he was trying to take away the most stability she'd had in years.

After her café in Leeds had shown the first signs of bottoming out, Mel had sold while the going was better than worse and decided to search out a new spot to move to. She'd had two rules in mind. One, the place had to have little to no competition. Two, after moving around for so many years, she finally wanted to find a place she would come to call home. So she'd packed up her life, headed south, and stumbled across Rabbits Leap after getting lost and motoring about inland Devon with a perilously low tank of petrol.

The moment she'd seen the pretty village filled with blooming flower boxes, kids meandering down the main street licking ice creams without parents helicoptering about them, and a store smack bang in the middle with a 'for rent' sign stuck to the door, a little part of her heart had burst into song. The plan had been to settle down, set up shop and make enough to save and survive. But, as she watched Tony flick through a fashion magazine, she could see her plans to make Rabbits Leap her forever home go the way of coffee dregs, down the drain.

She picked up the coffee and walked it over to Tony's table where he was stuffing his face.

'Your coffee.'

'Thish shcone is amazhing.' Tony swallowed and brushed crumbs from his lips and chin.

Full lips, strong angular chin, Mel noted, before mentally swatting herself. She wasn't meant to be perving on the enemy. 'Well, it's my grandma's secret recipe, so it should be.'

'Can I have the recipe?'

'What part of secret do you not understand?' She set the cup down with a clank.

'Sit.' Tony pushed out the chair opposite him with his foot.

'I've things to do.'

'Sit.'

Mel huffed, then did as she was told.

'So, how are things?' Tony picked up the cup and took a sip, giving a small grunt of appreciation.

'That's how good yours are going to have to be.' Mel folded her arms across her chest and tipped her head to the side. A small show of arrogance, but for all the things she wasn't great at, she knew she could cook and she could make a damn good cup of coffee.

'It's good to know the benchmark.' Tony's voice was strong but she was sure a hint of panic flashed through those blue sparklers of his. 'Anyway, this isn't about me. How are you? I haven't seen you in the pub with that vet of yours for a while now.'

Mel narrowed her eyes in suspicion. 'Have you been staking me out? Figuring all the ways you can try and horn in on my bit of business?'

'Rabbits Leap makes a habit of knowing Rabbits Leap. We keep an eye on our own. We take care of our own...' A tightening of those lush lips. A moment of regret? No matter. He'd given her ammunition.

'You take care of your own by taking over parts of their businesses? My, how civically minded you are.'

'I know you're annoyed about the machine, Mel, but you don't have to be sarcastic about it. Can't we deal with the situation like adults?'

Mel's grip around herself tightened as her irritation soared. 'I can be whatever I want in my café. And I can say whatever I want, however I want, especially when dealing with a coffee thief. What's next? You'll be calling my beans supplier? Good luck with that. They know what loyalty means.'

Tony's lips thinned out more. Good. She was getting to him. Giving him something to think about.

'As for the vet? Not that it's any of your business but we're over. He decided small-town veterinary work wasn't for him and headed over to Africa to work with wildebeest or something like that.'

'Thought he would.'

'Really?' Mel's chin lifted in surprise. She'd never thought Tony was the kind of guy who delved below the surface of anything. With that easy smile and light laugh, he seemed… well, about as shallow as one of the puddles that amassed on the main street after a spring shower.

'Yeah, he had that look about him, the "this place will do for now" look. I've seen it before. I knew it was only a matter of time before he left.' Tony picked up his coffee and took a sip. 'God, this really is good. Is everything you do this good?'

Mel's ears prickled hot. Was she imagining it or was that a double entendre? She met his blue eyes and saw not a hint of sparkle or tease. Nope, no double entendre; he wasn't trying to pick her up.

'I guess that means I was "this girl will do for now",' she said out loud, more to herself than to Tony.

'Then he was a fool. A man would be lucky to have a pink-haired barista and amazing cook loving him, cooking for him and making his morning coffee.'

'That sounds more like a slave-master relationship than a real, true-love one…'

'I'm sure the man would repay you in other ways.'

This time the sparkle was definitely in his eyes.

'I'd make sure he did.' The words came out before she could stop them, along with a wink. *Traitor.* She dipped her head to hide the flush creeping up over her cheeks. How dare her body flirt so easily with the enemy, even though, with his kind words, he was acting more like a friend. Or someone who might be angling for something more than that. Not that she'd ever sleep with the enemy. Uh-uh. No way.

Taking a long, slow, cooling breath she looked up into Tony's eyes. Something flashed through them. Something quick, hot, fierce. A heck of a lot like desire. Had he been thinking about her… with him? Mel shook the thought clear. Nope, that'd never happen. They were chalk and cheese. Besides, there was no way she was playing around with the local lothario. He didn't tick any of her boxes. Well, not all of them. Hot. Yes. Fun. Yes. But he couldn't commit. She'd heard the village gossip. He was a one-man band. No woman lasted more than a night. Anyway, he was hardly boyfriend material. He only loved himself, and he was obviously careless with money, which meant careless with security, and that was the one thing Mel was always careful about.

'So why did you come here, Tony?'

'I need to apologise and then we need to have a conversation.'

Mel sat up straighter in her chair. An apology? She hadn't seen that coming. 'So, apologise.'

'I'm sorry I bought the coffee machine. Actually, I'm not. But I'm sorry you had to find out about it like that.'

'Not much of an apologiser, are you?'

He at least had the good grace to look slightly ashamed.

'Well, I'm hoping we can come to an arrangement about it.'

'Really? How about I arrange for it to be removed and you go back to bartending?'

'How about you teach me how to use it… and maybe even teach me how to cook?'

Mel couldn't believe what she was hearing. Was Tony mentally deficient?

'Cook? What are you on?'

'That smell, what is it?'

Mel sniffed the air and remembered she had lamb shanks slow-cooking in a tomato balsamic jus in the back kitchen.

'That's my dinner.'

'It smells amazing.'

'Don't try and distract me.' She waved her hand in impatience. 'Why would I teach you my whole trade? Coffee and baking? I'd be out of business within weeks.'

'No, I don't want to know how to bake. I'm talking about learning to cook real food, like whatever it is you've got going back there.' Tony's eyes sparkled with excitement.

Mel could almost see the ideas forming in his head. His whole demeanour was changing in front of her eyes, energy sparking off his disturbingly muscular body.

'You've seen the food we do at The Bullion. It's all deep-fried and artery-clogging. I need to get with the times, update the menu, make it appealing, *maybe* even get entertainment in on special nights, see if I can't pull in a few more punters. Turn the place into a tourist attraction, or something. Which would be good for your business, too...'

Tony leaned forward and placed his hand over hers.

Pull away.

But she couldn't. Tony's fingers tightened around the outer edges of her fist, warm, strong, capable. Hands that knew how to work. Weren't afraid of getting dirty...

Did he work out, she mused, as her eyes travelled up the length of his legs and settled on his stomach. Was there a six-pack hiding beneath that grey T-shirt? Strongly defined, hard thighs underneath those denims? Biceps made for picking a woman up and pinning her to a wall...

Get it together, girl! She squeezed her eyes shut, hoping not seeing Tony would stop those unneeded images forming in her head. It didn't work. Was this the effect he had on women? Is that why he was known for having a string of them? Was he truly irresistible?

'So are you going to help me? Or are you too busy meditating over there?'

Mel tugged her hand out from under his and rubbed her face wearily. It had been a long day. Between her mother's announcement sending her stomach into free-fall and the revelation that the man sitting opposite her had decided to pit himself against her in the business stakes, she was ready to go to bed. Alone.

'What's in it for me?' Mel opened her eyes to see Tony giving her a charming smile.

'The pleasure of my company?'

'I'm not seeing anything pleasurable about your company.' The lie came quick and easy.

'Well, maybe it's time you did.' Tony's teasing tone was back. 'Look, how about this for a deal. You help me create a dinner menu, maybe show me how to make a decent coffee…'

Mel's eyebrows shot up, her hackles rising.

'…and I promise to not serve the java until your café closes at…'

'Three.'

'Three it is.'

'I still don't feel like it's a good enough deal for me to give you this much help…'

'Any wine you drink at the pub will be free for the duration of your help?'

The teasing tone was tinged with desperation. Tony had alluded to things not going great, things needing fixing, but maybe he was in deeper than he was willing to let on? And maybe – an idea flitted about her mind – he could help her with her latest drama, the drama that was about to blow into town any day now…

'Okay. I'm insane for doing this, I'll probably regret it with every fibre of my being, but okay. I'll help you… but you've got to do one more thing for me.'

'Anything. Just name it.'

Mel screwed up her courage and forced the words out before she could talk herself out of them. 'I need you to be my fiancé.'

CHAPTER TWO

The scrape of metal on wooden floor filled the café as Tony pushed the chair away from the table and sprang up. 'Woah, hold on there, Mel. You're moving a little fast for me. Learning a few tips and tricks in the kitchen in exchange for getting married? I usually like to have a couple of dates first, be given flowers, chocolates, maybe even a diamond ring…' he joked, hoping to see her demeanour lighten up.

He waited for Mel's shoulders to sink. They didn't. He looked for her serious eyes to lighten. They remained serious.

'Mel, this is the bit where you lightly elbow me in the stomach and tell me you're joking.'

Mel stood up and folded her arms over her chest. 'But I'm not joking. You need to be my fiancé if you want me to teach you how to cook. It's this deal or no deal.'

Tony levelled his gaze at Mel. What was she playing at? 'You're dreaming, Mel. Literally. I don't do girlfriends. And I don't do fiancées. Ever. There's not a girl in this world who could make me settle down.'

Mel clapped a hand to her forehead and groaned. 'Oh my God, not a real fiancé, you crazy man. There's no way I'd put my heart in your hands, I've heard what people say about you, you know.'

Tony shrugged, unabashed. He knew what people said about him. It was the truth. He didn't stick around, and he didn't make promises he couldn't keep. His father had shown him what heartbreak looks like, and he didn't want to be in the position to repeat it. That meant love was off the table.

'I don't understand. Why do you need a fake fiancé? What for? To get back at the vet? The one who's on a whole other continent, probably with his arm up a rhino's butt right now?'

Mel closed her eyes as if trying to centre herself. 'God, she's not even here and I'm being sucked into her maelstrom,' she mumbled under her breath.

'Her? Who's her?' He took a step away from Mel. Then another. The café's door was only a few metres away; maybe he could make his escape and forget any of this had ever happened. He'd find another way to save The Bullion, to keep it out of some grabby, money-hungry estate agents' hands. Maybe he'd just have to return the coffee machine? Get the money back. Pay the rates. But then what? There'd only be more rates to come, and no money to pay them. No. He had to think bigger. He had to do everything in his power to attract the locals back, and to maybe even attract those from nearby villages.

Mel bit down on her lip. '*Her* is my mother. I need a fake fiancé for when my mother arrives.' She opened her eyes and met his gaze. Didn't even flinch when he gave her his best 'are you for real?' look.

'So let me get this straight. In exchange for teaching me to cook proper pub food and for letting me serve coffee after 3p.m., I have to be your fake fiancé for the duration of your mother's stay? I just don't think it's worth it. I'm getting the pointier end of the stick.'

'Well, it's not like we'd have to live together. And she'd only be here a few days. Mum never stays anywhere very long. And, well, I hate to say this, Tony, but you need me. I've heard the rumours. Mrs Harper was in here today saying The Bullion isn't paying its bills, and that it's also behind in taxes. That you're only months away from being bankrupt and losing everything. Let me help you change that. And I promise that, once my mother has gone, I'll release you from fiancé duties and continue to help you build a menu.'

Tony pinched the bridge of his nose. Damn. He'd hoped people hadn't realised the dire straits he was in. But with his dad's refusal to admit they were in trouble, then the cost of his funeral, and on top of that the modernisations and innovations of pubs in the closest villages, which had seen Rabbits Leap's locals leaving The Bullion for more interesting pastures, money had been tight. Tighter than tight. Verging on non-existent. He was screwed. And Mel knew it.

'So, Tony McArthur, will you marry me?'

Tony's breath caught in his throat, like a noose round his neck, or a ring on his finger. 'It seems I have no choice.'

'Good.' Mel nodded. 'Well, it's time for me to shut up shop, so we may as well make a start. Have you ever made lasagne?'

***

Mel picked up one of Tony's knives and ran her finger over the blade. It was as blunt as she'd been back at the café. Her stomach had knotted up when she'd brought up his financial situation, but he'd left her no choice. She needed him as much as he needed her, and she didn't have the time to deal with his resistance, not with her mother due to arrive on her doorstep.

'When's the last time these were sharpened?' She turned to Tony who was propping open the door that separated the pub and kitchen, keeping an eye on the handful of punters who were nursing a beer.

He shrugged. 'Not since Dad passed. And even then, he wasn't one for the cooking. That had been Mum's domain.' He flicked his eyes away from her and focused them on the customers.

Was it her imagination or had Tony's eyes misted up?

'How old were you when your mum passed?'

'Five.'

'That must have been hard, not having her around.' Mel rifled through a drawer and found a butcher's steel and got to work sharpening the knife in preparation for her first cooking lesson.

Tony glanced down at his shoes and grunted. Followed by another shoulder shrug.

So it had been hard. Mel figured as much. She knew a thing or two about not having parents around, and she didn't know what was worse. Having one gone forever, or having one who came and went whenever it suited them...

She set the steel down and grabbed an onion. 'Right, so you know how to chop an onion, don't you?'

'Of course I do. Pass the knife.'

Mel sighed, relieved. Since she'd followed him to the pub he'd been all monosyllabic answers and grunts. That, combined with furtive glances and plenty of space between the two of them, had made for an uncomfortable half hour. How they were going to fake a relationship in front of her mother she had no idea, but maybe the cooking would bring them together.

'Stop!' she cried out, registering the butchering going on in front of her. 'What are you doing to that poor vegetable? What did it ever do to you?'

'What do you mean, what am I doing? I'm chopping it up like you said.'

'You're killing it deader than dead. Who even thought to teach you how to chop a vegetable like that?'

'Well, as we just talked about, my mother has been busy being deceased for the last couple of decades and my father's idea of cooking involved a deep fryer and whatever came out of the bulk bags of bar food he had shipped in. So what little I know is what I've taught myself.'

Mel's face flashed crimson-hot with embarrassment. 'I'm sorry. Stupid choice of words.'

'Don't worry about it.' The deep lines running between Tony's eyes softened. 'So, are you going to show me how to cut an onion or are you going to just stand there looking at me with that cute little face of yours all red as those tinned tomatoes?'

'First rule of the kitchen – don't irritate the chef by calling her cute. Now give me that knife.'

Mel took the knife off Tony, grabbed a fresh onion, chopped the top off it, halved it, then began running the knife down the length of it, making lines half a centimetre apart. When she reached the other end of the onion she spun it round and efficiently sliced it width-wise, watching with satisfaction as little cubes of onion crumbled onto the board.

'It's like magic.'

The wonder in Tony's voice made her grin. It had seemed a little like magic to her the first time she'd watched a chef do it, too, but after peeling and chopping her thousandth onion in a matter of weeks it had well and truly stopped feeling magical and simply felt like second nature.

She ran her finger down the blade of the knife to clean off the last few bits of onion, then flipped the handle in Tony's direction.

'Your turn.'

Tony glanced sceptically at the knife, then turned the look on her.

'It won't bite,' she said.

'But you might.'

'Not if you don't want me to…' Her words came out low, sweet… and there was no missing the seductive tone. Mel mentally kicked herself in the shins. What was going on with her? She was acting like… someone she never wanted to act like.

Tony's lips quirked as his eyebrow raised in amusement. 'Geez, Mel. Is it getting hot in here, or is it just me?'

The sparkle was back, sending the warmth that had bloomed over Mel's face skyrocketing. 'Yeah, it's hot. It's just the oven. Another rule – if a recipe says preheat the oven, preheat the oven.' She fanned her face furiously. 'That's a mighty good oven you've got over there. Works fast.' *Stop burbling*, she ordered herself. 'Now stop gawking at me, pick up the knife and chop that onion like I showed you.'

'Yes, Ma'am.' Tony saluted and took the knife from her.

He held it gently, as if it might bite. The complete opposite to the confident manner with which he'd grabbed it before hacking at the onion a few minutes ago.

'Chop off the top,' Mel instructed, keeping her voice soft, calm, so as not to freak him out any more.

His fingers took hold of the fresh onion and held it to the board. His knuckles turned more and more white with tension the closer the knife got to its victim. His shoulders bunched up once more.

'You don't have to be nervous. You've got this. You can do it. It's just chopping an onion. I mean, you did it before, badly, but you did it.'

The knife clattered loudly onto the stainless-steel bench as Tony took an abrupt step back.

'What's wrong? You'll be fine.'

She reached out to touch his arm but he jerked it away so it was just out of reach.

'I don't know. I don't know if I can do this. What if I bugger it up? What if it all goes wrong?' His blue eyes were panicked as the words rushed out.

Mel knew he wasn't talking about the onion. He had the look of a person who could see their future falling apart. His voice held the same fear she'd felt to her very core when her business in Leeds had started to fall over. His eyes had the same wild look she'd seen reflected back at herself every time she'd been packed up, pulled out of school and taken somewhere to start a new life.

His life was spinning out of control and he didn't believe he could do a single thing to slow it down. But she could.

'Here. I'll help.' She picked up the knife. 'We'll do it together.'

Mel faced the bench and indicated for him to get behind her. Tony nodded in understanding and encircled her with his arms. One hand fell atop of her onion-holding hand, the other her knife-holding hand.

'Relax.' She wriggled her knife-holding hand, the hand he was currently squeezing every last drop of blood out of.

'Sorry,' he grunted, loosening his grip.

Mel focused on the onion and tried to ignore the tension she could feel radiating off him. Tension, and heat, and the slightest aroma of salt mixed with a hoppy earthiness. He smelt like a man should. Raw. Pure. Her body swayed backwards a little, closer to him. A mind of its own, it wanted to feel him against her, to see if they were a good fit.

Snap out of it. She wasn't here to have a fling with the town playboy, she was here to work, to show him how to make a simple lasagne, and that was it.

'So we chop the head off the onion.'

She pressed down on the knife, feeling him press along with her, his hand hot upon hers.

'Then we cut it in half.'

They swivelled the onion round and sliced through it, the two halves separated, releasing its potent aroma.

'Now you peel the layers off,' she instructed, momentarily feeling bereft when his hands left hers.

'Now we slice down the length.'

His hands were on hers again. She couldn't ignore the way his touch sent tingles racing up her arms, through her body, upsetting a flutter of butterflies that had been hibernating in her stomach. Was she really this desperate for a man? Did she need one so much that the tiniest hint of touch, the smallest flash of interest, sent her into a swooning mess?

'Have you forgotten how to cut an onion?'

His breath was hot on her ear. The butterflies danced again.

'Of course not. I was just taking it slowly…' She fished around for an excuse. 'Um, so, you know, *you* don't forget how to cut an onion.'

'So shouldn't we be cutting down the width of it now?'

His fingers interlaced with hers and turned the onion around, before lifting the knife and cutting through the vegetable, sending little squares tumbling. Tumbling like her willpower. All she had to do was turn around, one hundred and eighty small, tight degrees, and she would be face to face, body to body, heart to heart, with a man she was damn sure could make her forget about her earlier phone call, about what was to come.

She let out a shaky breath.

'Are you okay down there?' Tony's words were smooth, gentle. They mirrored the way she'd spoken to him earlier, when she'd had to bring him down from whatever fears he faced.

'Fine. I just…' She trailed off, unsure whether she could trust Tony, whether he would understand how one person could turn your world upside down, could shake things up, could leave you scrambling to put together the pieces for years after. Perhaps even a lifetime.

The slam of The Bullion's heavy, oak front door hitting the wall followed by the dull rumble of feet on threadbare carpet snapped Mel out of her reverie. 'Oh my God, it sounds like a whole rugby team just barged in…'

'Oh, shit. Bollocks.' Tony pushed her arm, still wrapped round him, away and crossed the kitchen to the bar in two long strides. 'It's not the sound of rugby players. It's actual rugby players.'

Mel moved to where he was standing and watched as a wave of slightly overweight middle-aged men rushed to the bar. 'What kind of rugby team are they?'

'The kind that come every second year for the annual grudge match. It's this weekend. The Randy Rabbits vs The Bad Boys of Babbler. And the opposition are meant to be staying at The Bullion.'

'And you forgot this?' Mel looked up at Tony and registered the shock on his face, emphasised by the slight shade of green his skin was giving off.

'How the hell did I forget? I can't send them away, I need their cash,' Tony said to no one in particular. 'The beds aren't made. I didn't order extra food. I don't even have anyone who can help me out at the bar. Jody's busy with the boys…'

Tony glanced down at Mel. 'But you. You're here. You could help me. You're my fiancée, after all.'

Mel shook her head and backed away from the madman in front of her. 'That's not part of the deal. That's not what I signed up for. And besides, I have to be in bed soon. I've got a business to run, too, remember? And I have to be up early to bake.'

'You promised, Mel. You promised you'd help me save The Bullion. And look, there's a whole team of hungry men out there. And we're making a lasagne. We've got the ingredients. You just have to do that… and then maybe sort out the bedrooms for me. Come on, Mel. You're my fiancée. You have to.' Tony reached for her hands and held them in his to his heart, which she could feel thumping through his navy jumper. 'Don't make me beg. It's just… there's no one else.'

There's no one else.

Damn it. Couldn't he have chosen another line? Mel knew all too well what it was like to have to fend for yourself. There was no way she could turn him down.

'Fine,' she sighed. 'But you're still cooking the lasagne. I'll finish off the onions while you get that lot out there sorted for drinks, all right?'

She waved him off and went back to prepping dinner, the chopping and dicing soothing her jangled nerves.

Between her new and unexpected attraction to Tony and her mother's impending arrival she was out of sorts. Gone was her perfectly ordered life of waking up, baking, serving customers, then reading or watching a show and going to bed. Instead, here she was, teaching a man to cook a lasagne, offering to make beds, and trying her best to help out the one person who'd threatened her security in the first place.

But it was all for the greater good. It had to be.

She scraped together the onions and waited for Tony to come back in to finish off his first cooking lesson. And waited. Then waited some more. Impatient to get going, she poked her head through the door to see him pulling pint after pint. His usually artfully mussed hair was standing out at odd angles, and a sheen of perspiration covered his forehead.

Tony glanced over and caught her eye. 'I'll be through in a minute.'

'You don't look like you'll get away at the rate they're drinking.'

'Can you finish it off?'

'No. That's not the deal. You cook. I'll pour the drinks.'

'But I'm a barman. You're a cook.'

'And you're meant to be learning to cook. I've got the recipe written down. You just need to follow it. I'll be here if you need me.'

Tony's eyes narrowed. 'Do you even know how to pull a pint?'

'I've been dragged to enough pubs that I'm pretty sure I can copy what I've seen.' Mel picked up a glass and poured the perfect beer with just the right amount of head to prove her point.

'Fine. But soon as I'm done you're making the beds and I'm back on the bar.'

'Fine.' Mel waved him back to the kitchen, and tried to ignore the tingle of pleasure that bloomed and spread through her when he smiled his thanks.

***

Two hours later the last sheet was tucked in, the last comforter brushed smooth, the last pillow plumped, the last decent fingernail she had on her hands was well and truly ripped to shreds, and each and every last muscle in her body ached.

Mel stretched, hearing cricks and creaks throughout her shoulders and neck. That was a mission, and now she needed a drink. Luckily she was in a pub. And from the rousing chorus of the national anthem going on downstairs, things were still in full flight.

She plodded down the stairs and pushed through the staff door to see Tony hunched over the bar, his head in his hands, half or even mostly asleep.

'Any chance of an Irish crème and milk?' she whispered softly in his ear, not wanting to startle him.

'Any chance of you sorting yourself out?' he mumbled into his hands.

She thought to remind him that she'd been up since the early hours, that she'd poured loads of beer and then served up the lasagne he'd cooked to a whole rugby team, and then made up twenty beds, but thought better of it. This wasn't the Tony the ladies of the village liked to gossip about over their lattes. That Tony had an easy smile, a carefree attitude and, once in the sack, had all the energy of a spring bunny. This Tony? He looked shattered. Beaten. More in need of a good sleep than a roll in the hay.

Mel glanced over at the gleaming monstrosity. Although now that he'd promised not to step on her turf, the coffee machine didn't seem quite so evil. And right now it could come in handy. She walked down to the end of the bar, ignoring the catcalls as some of the team realised there was a woman in their midst. She stood in front of it and ran her hand along the cool, gleaming steel. Switch on, pour milk in jug, and steam. The ritual was as soothing as ever. She frothed the milk so it was just warm, not hot. Then, pouring it into a mug, she took it down to Tony.

'Here.' She pressed the cup against the back of his hand.

He jolted in fright.

'You need this.'

'Does it have caffeine in it?' He turned his head and gave her a sleepy half-smile. 'Because I really need caffeine. A truckload of it.'

'If you're going to be dealing with this rabble...' She nodded towards the players who, for some unknown reason, had decided to build a human pyramid. 'You're going to need a good sleep. Take it. It's just warm milk.'

'You're too good to me.' He took the mug in one hand and cupped her cheek with the other.

'Well. If that's not love's dream right there, I don't know what is!'

Mel froze. She knew that voice. Brash. Loud. Demanding. That voice wasn't meant to be here until tomorrow. She jerked her head away from Tony's hand, mortified to be caught in such a tender, intimate moment...

'Are you just going to stand there looking like a gormless wonder, or are you going to get your behind over here and give your mother a hug?'

Hurricane Val had hit.

CHAPTER THREE

'Mum, I didn't expect you so soon. What a surprise.'

Mel didn't look surprised; she looked shell-shocked, maybe even a little sick. Strange, you'd have thought she'd have been happy to see her mother.

Although to be fair, outside of their friendly chats over the bar and in passing on the street, Tony didn't know much about Mel. In fact he could tick off what he did know about her on one hand. She worked hard, kept to herself, and was pretty to look at. Pretty, and funny, and not afraid of getting stuck in and making things happen. He looked down at the warm milk she'd pressed into his hands. She was caring, too, but most definitely not his type. She was the settling type.

Or was she? A thought nagged at him… settling types liked their family, didn't they? Wanted to have them around? Have a big one themselves? Breed like rabbits and enjoy big family dinners every night? Cheerful Christmases. Rowdy birthdays. So Mel's mother turning up should've been a good thing. So why was Mel going so pale that her black-and-pink hair was looking both darker and more vibrant than ever?

'Mel, aren't you going to introduce me to your handsome friend? I'm sure I raised you better than that.' Mel's mother thrust her hand forward, palm down, in Tony's direction.

She wanted him to kiss her hand? Not shake it? And had she just thrown him a flirtatious wink along with that girlish giggle?

'The name's Tony.' He leant over and kissed her proffered hand, making Mel's mum laugh in delight as she flipped her poker-straight, long blonde hair over her shoulder. Out of the corner of his eye he could see Mel shake her head and roll her eyes. So she *wasn't* her mother's number-one fan. Odd.

'And I'm Valerie. It's a pleasure to meet you.'

'What made you come early, Mum? And why all the bags? I thought you were only planning to stay for a day or two.'

Tony followed Mel's gaze to the bags stacked by the front door. There were so many, Mel's mum could've started up her own luggage shop.

A knot began to form in his stomach.

'Oh, Mel, let's not talk about that right now. We can catch up properly tomorrow. What I need right now is my beauty sleep. Where's the nearest bed?'

Did Mel's mum just give him a meaningful glance? Oh,

hell. There was no way he was sharing his bed with her. She'd eat him alive. Oh, and he was meant to be getting married to her daughter.

'My apartment's just down the road, Mum. You can sleep there.'

'Your apartment?' The flirty eyes hardened. 'You're engaged, aren't you? Why would you need an apartment? Surely you and your fiancé are living together?'

'We are.' The words came out before he could think. The knot grew tighter. Damn. Not enough sleep had made him stupid, unable to think straight. But it was too late to back out now. 'But sometimes this place gets rowdy late into the night and Mel has to be up early for the café, so that's when she stays over there.'

'Well, that's a very modern arrangement you've got going. Not particularly cosy, though. I don't know, Melanie… if I were getting married to this hunk right here I wouldn't let him out of my sight. Especially with so many women no doubt just waiting to pounce.'

'I trust Tony. He would never let me down. Unlike some people I know.'

Tony had spent enough hours watching people get tetchy with each other after a few drinks to know when he heard loaded words. Fighting words. Words to wind up the evening with before the two women got even more wound up and a full-on family spat erupted with a gleeful audience to egg them on. Tony ducked down and grabbed the megaphone he kept on hand for the rare occasion when the pub was busy and the patrons needed to be moved on. It was time for a bit, or a lot, of distraction.

'Down those drinks, boys. It's time to hit the sack!'

Tony ignored the groans and mutterings of 'killjoy' coming from the players.

Setting the megaphone down, he turned to Mel and Valerie. His booming announcement had stopped the sniping but Mel was still glaring at her mother, while her mother stared back at her daughter, an innocent expression on her face. He was mighty glad not to be sharing a room with either of them tonight. 'That goes for you two as well. Get home and I'll see you tomorrow.'

'You're shutting up shop? But I just got here.' Valerie pouted and widened her eyes. 'And you're sending the men away? Oh, surely we can stay up for one little drink. They look like so much fun.'

'What about your beauty sleep, Mum?' Mel asked pointedly.

'Oh, I'll just get it at the other end of the day. A good sleep-in works wonders… and besides, those gentlemen don't look ready for sleep either.'

'You'd have thought you'd have had enough fun for a lifetime.' Mel's tone was as dark as the shadows under her eyes.

'Sorry, Valerie. Once the megaphone has come out, it's time for everyone to get out.'

'Well, you can't blame a girl for trying.' Valerie smiled prettily up at him. 'Speaking of trying… Melanie, you really ought to do something with that hair of yours. Honestly. It's hardly feminine.'

Tony watched Mel's chest rise as she sucked in a breath, then slowly deflated. Counting to ten? Twenty? Her mother had been here only a few minutes and she'd already insulted Mel twice. No wonder they weren't close.

'My hair's fine, Mother. Now let's get going. I've got to be up early and you're not the only one who needs beauty sleep.'

'Oh, I can see that, dear. Don't you worry.' Valerie turned to Tony. 'It was a pleasure meeting you. I can't wait for us to get further acquainted.'

Tony caught Mel rolling her eyes and winked at her as she gathered up as many bags as she could while her mother took one in each hand. As they tottered out the door Mel slung her mother a murderous look.

A sigh of relief escaped his lips. Right, so he had one night to figure out how to be a convincing fiancé for a few days. He remembered the towering suitcases. At least, he hoped it would only be for a few days…

**

'This is a very homely apartment you've got here, Melanie.'

Homely? In her mother's vernacular that meant 'pokey'.

45

'I like it.' And she did. The apartment above the shop was small, but it was all she needed. Open-plan living with a small kitchenette, one bedroom, and a bathroom. The landlord had allowed her to splash a little paint on the walls. And although lemon yellow wasn't everyone's cup of tea, she liked it. It reminded her of the bedroom she'd spent so much time in at her grandma's.

'And there's an awful lot of stuff here for a spot where you just need to sleep...'

God, the Spanish Inquisition would've been easier to deal with. Nothing got past Valerie. She had a knack of sizing someone up and seeing their weak spots, or the secrets they were hiding, in seconds. She wasn't afraid to let them know about it either. Like Tony and the drunken women...

'Well, Tony's living area isn't exactly large...'

'But he has a huge building? Surely he could take over one of the pub's bedrooms, maybe knock a wall out and create some room for you? I mean, you've been together how long now? At least a year?'

Mel groaned inwardly. Lying to her mother about her relationship status had seemed like a good idea at the time, a way to stop the constant badgering about settling down with a man. She'd kind of hoped the vet was going to become the real-life embodiment of her fake boyfriend, but that hope left when he did. And the last thing she'd expected was her mother to visit. That wasn't something they did... well, apart from the times when something had gone wrong in her mother's life... which begged the question, why was she here? What had gone wrong?

'Yeah... we've been going out just over a year now.' Mel felt the walls starting to close in on her. Her previously cosy apartment now felt like it was about to choke her.

'Well, he really needs to sort that situation out. I'll talk to him. I can't have my girl living out of a suitcase.'

Air. There was none. The world was starting to spin. Mel walked to the window, pushed it open and breathed in the brisk, wintry air. Although tinged with wood smoke it felt fresh, clearing, invigorating.

'And don't tell me you're pregnant? Have you set a date for the wedding? We'll move it up. I don't want my only child to be an unwed mother, or worse, look like a marshmallow in a wedding dress.'

Mel spun to her mother, anger pulsing in her veins. What right did she have to come in here and tip her nice, secure, routined-up-the-yin-yang life upside down? Hadn't she done that enough?

'Mother. I'm not pregnant. I'm just tired. I've been up since the wee hours. I've worked all day in the café. Then worked all night for Tony. And look, it's the wee hours again. I need to get some sleep. And I don't need to be harangued about every aspect of my life...'

Her mother's soft-blue eyes welled up with tears. Of course, she was able to give it but not take it. Nothing had

47

changed there. But despite everything, seeing her mother in pain tugged at her heart. Same way it always had.

'After all, there's plenty of time for you to do that.' She lifted one eyebrow and gave her a small, teasing smile, glad to see the tears recede as fast as they'd built up.

'Oh, Mel.' Her mother swept over and pulled her into her lean embrace. 'What a mean old cow you must think I am. I only want the best for you. It's all I've ever wanted.'

You wanted the best for me? Mel was glad her mother couldn't see the grimace on her face. When had she ever wanted the best for her?

'Now, since you're not with child, you sleep on this perfectly comfortable-looking couch and I'll take your bed.' She felt a kiss brush the top of her head. 'There's a good girl.'

***

Ting-a-ling. Ting-a-ling. Ting-a-ling.

'You kids stop playing with the door before I throw an overcooked muffin at your heads. Now get out of here and get to school,' Mel yelled, searching for a pen underneath the sofa where customers usually waited for their takeaway coffees.

'Nice arse!'

Mel nearly hit her head in shock. What kid in town had a baritone voice, let alone the cheek to say that to her?

'Woohoo! Breakfast and a show!'

'You lot. Cut that out. Show the lady some respect. She's about to cook you the finest breakfast you've ever had.'

Mel wiggled her way backwards from under the sofa and stood up, clutching the pen. She smiled gratefully at Tony, who was staring in irritation at the rugby team as they piled into the café, their big frames filling up her chairs and tables, their aroma of deodorant and sweat competing with the aroma of freshly baked bread.

What was that look all about? And why were his fists clenched? Because they'd gone all caveman on her? Was he...? She flicked the idea away. No. Surely not. He couldn't be jealous... just acting jealous, in case her mother was around. Acting like an overprotective fiancé. And speaking of her mother... was she still in bed?

Mel checked the time on the whitewashed reindeer clock on the wall that was surrounded by retro mirror art. Just past ten and she was still sleeping? She'd hoped she might have the decency to come and give her a hand this morning, maybe put together a few paninis or ice a cake, but no, that would mean Valerie was doing something for someone else for a change. And since helping her daughter out would serve no benefit to her, it was never going to happen. Mel gritted her teeth in self-directed irritation. When would she stop giving her mother the benefit of the doubt?

Tony placed his hand on Mel's shoulder and gave it a small squeeze. 'Are you going to keep perving on the players or are you going to thank me?'

Mel considered shrugging his hand off. With no mother about there was no reason to act all touchy-feely with each other, but it felt warm, safe…possessive. Like he actually cared for her well-being. The hand on shoulder could stay, she decided. 'Thank you for what? Bringing business into the café or giving me a cheap thrill? It's nice to know my "arse" is still considered "nice", even if the compliment came from a guy who I'm pretty sure might be closely related to a Neanderthal.'

Mel met Tony's eyes. The irritation had abated, but she couldn't miss the way he kept flicking his gaze between her and the players, as if making sure they were ignoring her, showing the lady 'some respect'. Maybe he was being territorial? Or maybe he simply didn't like women being treated like meat. Perhaps there was more to Tony than just a good time.

'Thanks for defending my honour back there.' She resisted the temptation to bat her eyelashes and add 'my hero'. The last thing she needed to do was make the mess they were in even more muddled by flirting with Tony.

'Well, I couldn't have my betrothed being admired by other men and not say something. It would be unseemly. Um, small question, Mel…' He lowered his voice and dropped his head closer to hers. 'How are we going to explain our engagement to the town? Because I get the feeling your mother will not be discreet about it...'

Bugger. Mel hadn't thought about that. She hadn't really thought any of it through. Her heart began to race. What had she been thinking, coming up with such a mad-hat idea? She should've just agreed to help Tony with his business and told her mother a white lie about her fiancé being out of town for work. Now she was stuck with a fiancé known for being a commitment-phobe and a mother who would probably marry them right then and there if she could. Her mother's obsession with marriage was a mystery to Mel, but ever since she'd been born, that was all she'd done – meet and marry, meet and marry – and for some reason, despite its never having worked for her, she thought her daughter should do the same. Mel inwardly grimaced. It wasn't like she had anything against marriage, but if she was going to do it she was going to do it right, with the right man, not the kind of men her mother had shacked up with.

'Okay, okay okay.' The words came quick, hurried. Tinged with heart-pumping panic. 'We need to sort this out, now.'

She grabbed Tony by his shirt and pulled him behind the counter, ignoring the 'you get 'em' cheers of the rugby players who seemed to think they were witnessing a passionate moment.

Ow! Her ankle caught on the metal leg of her kitchen

table and she lost her balance, sending them falling backwards. She prepared for a second wave of pain as her back headed towards the lip of the stainless-steel bench. Instead, it was cushioned by something warm and soft, yet strong. Tony's arms, she realised, as she saw a twinge of pain hit his eyes.

'Are you okay?' he asked, furrows of concern appearing between his brows. 'Did you hurt yourself?'

A stray blond curl flopped onto his forehead. It looked so silky. She fought the urge to reach up, wrap it around her fingers to discover whether it was as silken as she suspected, whether it would spring up if she pulled it down and released.

'Are you winded? Are you in a whole heap of pain? You're looking pretty dazed right now.'

She focused on his lips. Full, soft, yet no doubt capable of being hard, passionate. If she just stood on tippy toes she'd be able to reach those lips… be able to kiss them…

'Should I be calling an ambulance?'

She blinked. Once. Twice. A handful of times. What had she been thinking? Kissing Tony? Was she mental? That'd only complicate an already messy situation.

'I'm… fine.'

She was also dry. Who knew a hot wave of lust could make you so thirsty. She turned around in his arms, reached over for a glass and…

Hello. She felt something prod against her lower back.

Hard. Thick. Long. Something that had a reputation for pleasing women far and wide. Should she pretend she had no idea? That'd be the polite thing to do. She grabbed a glass, filled it with water and turned back to Tony, who still hadn't released her from his grasp. Not that she was complaining.

She sipped the water. Watching him watching her as the cool water wet her lips. Beaded on them.

His throat worked as he tried to swallow. Who knew Tony, stud of the land, could get so het up?

'Water?' She offered him the tumbler. 'You look like you need it.' She glanced down at the bulge-fest. 'Feels like you need it, too.'

A slow smile spread over Tony's face. *Damn it.* She should've kept her mouth shut. Zipped it up and glued it for good measure. But this ridiculous, simmering attraction that kept flaring between them made her feel reckless. She closed her eyes. If she stared at those lips, that smile, that face one second longer she'd lose all control.

She was not going to lose control. Kissing her fiancé was not an option.

The glasses in the kitchen cabinet began to rattle as a soft footfall grew louder. Her mother was up, and coming down the stairs. Mel breathed a sigh of relief. Good. For once her timing was perfect.

'Morning, Mum,' she called, bright and cheery while trying to disentangle herself from Tony.

'Morn…' Valerie stopped short as she surveyed the scene before her.

Mel knew what it looked like. Two lovers caught in a clinch. A good thing, perhaps? At least it made their relationship look real.

Valerie's hand flew to her eyes, shielding them from sight. 'Oh! Don't let me stop you, you little lovebirds. Enjoying a touch of romance in the morning. How adorable! Go on… I'll just be making a cup of tea. Don't let me interrupt you.' She dropped her hand and gave them a wink, before flicking on the kettle.

'Oh, we're fine, Mum. We were just in the middle of discussing work stuff.' Mel made to duck out from under Tony, who only tightened his grip, a lazy smile spreading over his face.

Why wasn't Tony letting her go? All he had to do was take a step back and they'd be free from the madness. Or she could push him away. That was an option. A good one. Yes, she should do that. Except if she did that her mother would know something was up.

'Mel, I've been around long enough not to be embarrassed by a little kissing. Don't stop on my account. Besides, it's good for me to see my daughter in love. I was starting to think you were going to turn into a spinster like your grandmother.'

Had her mother gone soft in the head? Her grandmother had once been married and completely in love with her grandfather. Sure, he'd passed away at a young age and she'd never remarried, but she'd experienced true love and didn't feel the need to. Unlike Valerie, who clung to anything and anyone that might look like love, whether they were or not. Mel tensed, ready to remind her mother of those facts. Then stopped. Shocked into silence as something soft yet rough licked at her bottom lip. Lingered. Meandered over the soft curve.

Heat pooled in her lower stomach. Liquid yearning. She should put a stop to this right now. It would be the prudent thing to do. It would be...

Her lower lip was encased in heat. Oh God, this was happening; Tony was kissing her, engulfing her with his own lips.

He was spicy and salty and that aroma of hops was on his lips, too. She idly wondered if that delicious scent inhabited other areas of his body.

'Mel,' he whispered into her mouth. 'Don't forget to kiss me back.'

They locked eyes, his smiling into hers as she wrapped her arms around his neck and brushed her lips against his, the action setting her nerves on fire. She caught his bottom lip in her teeth, nipping, then releasing, before capturing his mouth fully with hers.

A moan escaped her lips as she arched into him. Wanting him, right there, right then. Oh God, she was moaning in front of her mother. And someone else was moaning, too...

'Food!'

'We're hungry!'

Another moan. This time from Tony. And not one born of desire.

He released her. Leaving her cold. Adrift. Her head fuzzy, her body screaming at her to grab him, caress him. Have him.

'The ferals are hungry.'

His voice was raspy, guttural. The words harsh, matching her breathing. And his eyes? The want she'd seen in them extinguished. A moment of madness? Or just Tony being Tony? Unable to resist a good time? No matter. She had work to do.

'Can you take orders?'

'Sure.'

She passed him a pen and order book.

'Thanks.'

He made to leave, but turned back. A mischievous glint lighting up his face.

'Mel?'

'Hmmm?' She kept it short. Non-committal. Matched the casual tone to Tony's.

'We'll talk later, my love.'

With a wink he was gone.

'Any ice in that freezer of yours?' Valerie asked, her eyes wide with innocence. 'Looks like you need to cool down.'

Mel turned round and collapsed onto the sink. The

steel cooling her lust-fevered forehead. This was nuts. Bonkers. What was she doing playing around with the local lothario? And why was she letting her mother push her into it?

She was just asking for trouble. Asking to be left heartbroken and alone. She'd seen enough of that to last a lifetime. It was time to rein things in.

CHAPTER FOUR

Tony went to take another slurp of beer. Was it going to fix things? Nope. Bulk up his bank balance? Definitely not. Rid himself of this crazy situation? He very much doubted it. Would it take away that memory of him and Mel getting a little hot and heavy in her spotless kitchen? Maybe if he drank enough of it. But did he want to forget that? Hell, no.

Who knew little Miss Prim and Proper could be so unexpected, so sexy? Sure, she had that mad-hat pink-and-black-striped hair – that should've been a tip-off that there was a hint of wild child in her. But she'd always acted so serious. He'd never seen her put a foot wrong. There hadn't even been any village gossip about her, which in a village this small, with people just dying for titbits of scandal, was unheard of. Sure, the grapevine had buzzed with excitement when a café opened, painted in pink with green trim, fairy lights festooning the window outside, and a retro British vibe going on inside. But since then? Nothing. Zip. Even her brief relationship with the vet hadn't stirred up the gossip scene. If anything, people had commented that they were happy to see her with someone.

Tony could see why they'd been happy for her. Sure, she was always friendly, always smiling, but to his trained eye, used to sizing people up the moment they stepped through The Bullion's doors, Mel seemed lonely. Even though that smile reached her chocolatey-brown eyes, there was still a sadness that hung about the edges, a slight hardness, too, that told you to keep out, to enter at your own risk. Tony knew the moment she'd walked through his doors she was off limits. She wouldn't be one for his one-night ways. He protected his heart by keeping things light and easy; she protected hers by keeping people like him out. Although now, he wondered, after that intimate moment, were those barriers breaking?

'Are you ready for your next lesson?'

Mel. Damn. He'd forgotten he was meant to be learning how to get all Gordon in the kitchen. She was going to be annoyed. Super annoyed. Because from the looks of it she was already peeved about something. Irritation rippled off her, from those dainty feet clad in simple red trainers, all the way up her black jeans and black long-sleeved T-shirt. Her uniform. He was pretty sure even the stripes in her hair were glowing more vividly.

'What's got you so angry all of a sudden?' Tony cringed inwardly. That was a dumb thing to say. Never ask an angry person why they're angry. Especially if they look like they want to whack something with a frying pan. And doubly so if they have ready access to said frying pan.

'Doesn't matter.' Mel dumped her bag onto the bar. 'It's not your problem, not your business. Did you get the lamb shanks like I told you?'

She was going to kill him.

'Sorry. Forgot.'

Her hands flew to her hips. 'Why do I even bother? Honestly. It's like I'm surrounded by people who expect me to do all the work. To put in all the effort. If you can't just do your bit…'

'I'm sorry. Really.' Tony threw his hands up in apology, although he was beginning to think her anger wasn't necessarily aimed at him. Perhaps it was directed more at the blonde slip of a thing that had recently come to stay?

'Nope. I don't want to hear sorry, I've better things to do than waste my time with people who just want to do what they want to do. Go back to doing whatever you deemed so damn important that buying lamb shanks in order to save your business wasn't worth your time. Call me when you're ready to get serious. See you later.'

Mel turned on her heel and marched towards the door.

Really? She was just going to leave? In the mood she was in she'd snarl at every single one of her customers and put her own business in jeopardy, leaving them both high and dry. There was no way Tony was going to let that happen. Pushing the hinged door open he reached her in two easy strides. She squealed as he spun her round, picked her up by the waist and swung her over his shoulder, holding her there as she rained little fist-sized blows upon his back.

'Whack and wriggle all you want, Mel, but there's no way I'm letting you anywhere near my blunt set of knives while you're in a mood like this. And I'm not letting you storm through town. You'll scare your own customers off.'

Pushing The Bullion's door and propping it open with one leg, Tony stepped out into the pale winter sun. He knew what would calm Mel down. Or at the very least distract her from whatever or whoever had put her in such a foul mood.

'Where are you taking me? And put me down! You're acting like a caveman!'

'I was going for superhero,' Tony grinned as he carried her round to the back of the pub where his battered old pickup truck was stored.

'Well, I'm not a damsel in distress.'

The irritation was still in her voice but she'd stopped wriggling. Good, that was progress. He tightened his grip around her waist. She was so slim and bird-boned he half feared she would slip from his grasp onto the gravel driveway, something he'd hate to have happen, considering how much he was enjoying the view. Who knew her slightly too-big jeans had been hiding one of the most pert and perfectly formed rears he'd ever had the pleasure of seeing. His hand itched to move lower, to caress the rise and fall of her butt, to see if it felt as firm as it looked.

He gulped. Now was not the time to be getting frisky. Mel didn't need that. She needed a friend and, for some crazy reason he couldn't put his finger on, he wanted to try and be that person for her.

'You know you sounded pretty "woe is me" back there...'

'I was pissed off. Not "woe is me" – more "woe the person who crosses me right now".'

Tony laughed. 'Yeah, I got that feeling, too.'

He set her down on the driveway and smoothed her hair into place. Cupping her cheek he leant down, close enough to hear her slight intake of breath, to catch the faint hint of caramel, tinged with vanilla. The same heady combination he'd tasted earlier when they'd kissed.

'Now tell me, are you feeling better? Calmer? If I take you somewhere, are you going to growl at me about things I'm pretty sure I'm not responsible for? Like turning you into an evil villain in need of saving?'

Mel folded her arms across her chest and tipped her head to the side, eyes narrowed. 'So you're saying I'm not a damsel?'

'No, I was wrong.' Tony sized Mel up. She may be

slim and short, but she looked like she could take on the world if she had to. 'You're capable enough. Definitely not a damsel.'

'Well, then, I guess the answer to your question depends on where you're going to take me.'

'It's a surprise.' Tony smirked, enjoying having the upper hand for once. He opened the passenger door. 'Your carriage, my lady.'

Mel stood her ground and glared. 'You know I really do hate surprises.'

Yet she still took his outstretched hand and allowed him to help her up into the passenger seat of his old truck.

'It'd better be a good surprise.' She shot him a mutinous look.

'You're so cute when you're cross.'

Tony smiled as her glare wobbled, a small smile played about the corners of her mouth. He pushed the door shut and walked round to the driver's side, hopped in and turned the key, the engine making its usual noises of protestation before finally turning over. Good girl. *Don't fail me now. I've got another girl to make happy.*

'So... where are you taking me?'

It was the third time Mel had asked in as many minutes.

'Somewhere fun.' Tony cringed as the truck's gearbox made a grinding noise as he put it into fourth.

'Oh, come on. You keep saying that. Why can't you just tell me?'

Oh good. Mel the Irritated was back.

'Look, Mel, I know it was dumb of me to forget the lamb shanks, especially when I'm trying to keep my business going, but it didn't warrant that undressing. So, instead of taking whatever's got you riled up out on me, why don't you tell me what's wrong?'

'Nothing is wrong. Nothing I want to talk about anyway. Besides, you're only adding to the pile of things annoying me by not telling me where you're taking me. I don't like not knowing where I'm going.'

Tony shot a sideways glance at Mel. Her petite jaw was set and her eyes scoured the age-worn country road ahead with its bumps and potholes, flanked by untended hedgerows, as if looking for a safe spot to jump out.

'So does that mean you're not going to tell me what's really got you in a grump?' He kept his tone light, teasing, hoping it'd pull Mel out of her funk.

'I'm not in a grump,' she snapped.

Tony laughed. 'You so are. Denying it doesn't mean it's not true.'

Mel's tense shoulders slumped in defeat. 'Fine, I am in a grump. You'd better get used to it. Sorry.'

'I don't want to be engaged to an angry woman. And besides, it's a beautiful day. The last dump of snow has all but melted. There's a touch of heat in the sun. And look…' He pointed to the side of the road. 'An errant daffodil!

They're my favourite kind. You've got to love a flower that just pops up in amongst a whole bunch of weeds.'

'Someone would've had to put it there, I'm pretty sure.'

'Perhaps. But it keeps coming back. Year after year. It's resilient. A bit like you, I suspect.'

He glanced over at Mel. Her jaw, wound so tight before, had slackened. Even her pert little nose looked happier. What would it be like to kiss that nose? He shook his head. Now wasn't the time to be developing a nose fetish. Though hers was particularly cute.

'Oh!' Mel gasped and pointed. 'A bunny!'

Tony's usual reaction would've been to yell 'kill it' since they were considered pests, but seeing Mel bounce in the seat, her hands clapping in delight, he thought he'd leave it. She could be educated on the perils of rabbits another day.

'We're here.' He pulled into the driveway of his grandparents' home. Now, it belonged to him and Jody, though he considered it Jodes'.

When Jodes had come down with a case of the babies he'd told her to keep the farm. He was happy living at the pub. It was where their family had begun, where he'd learned about love, the good parts of it, and the sad. And he knew that this property, with its gently sloping hills, grazing animals and cosy cottage would be ideal for Jody and the kids. A place for their family to grow, for their family to love. And it was.

'Uncle Tony! Uncle Tony!'

Tyler and Jordan raced out of the house, their skinny legs and arms pumping hard. The smiles on their faces bringing a smile to his heart.

He pulled up and switched the truck's engine off just as they yanked open the door.

'What did you bring us, Uncle Tony?'

'Yeah, what did you bring us?' Jordan's eyes scoured the seat for treasures, no doubt of the sweet kind.

Whoops. Usually he had a treat for the boys, even if it was just a lollipop, but in his rush to cheer Mel up he'd clean forgotten. An idea sparked.

'Tyler, Jordan, I've brought you a new friend to play with.'

The boys looked over at Mel, disappointment written all over their faces.

'But she's a girl,' Tyler sniffed, rolling his eyes at Jordan.

'You won't think that's such a bad thing in a few years.' Tony grinned, ruffling his nephew's sandy-blond hair.

'Whatever.'

'Well, that's the present. Now go show Mel the lambs.'

'We had twins come the other day!' Jordan's eyes shone bright with excitement. 'Just like us.'

'Mum said we could keep them instead of killing them.' Tyler nodded his approval at the idea. 'Cool ay, Uncle Tony!'

'Very cool.'

'What's the girl's name?'

'The girl's name is Mel. Mel, I'd like you to meet my nephews. Tyler the Terrible and Jordan the Gigantic.'

'Uncle Tony! I'm bigger than Jordan and Mum says I'm more terrible, too.' Tyler placed his hands on his hips in indignation.

'Wouldn't be so proud of that fact if I were you.' Tony tugged Tyler's ear affectionately.

'Mel?' He turned to see Mel taking his two ruffian nephews in, her eyes weary. 'Don't prove the boys right. Go and show them how fun a girl can be.'

She turned her gaze on him. He didn't need to be a mind reader to know that those blunt knives of his were in danger of coming out when they got back to the pub's kitchen.

Her door opened.

'Come on, Mel.' Jordan held his hand out for her, ever the little gentleman that he was.

She hesitated a second, then took his hand and allowed him to help her down, her feet making a squishing sound as they sank into the soft mud.

'Jordan, can you get Mel a pair of your Mum's wellies while you're at it?'

'Sure thing, Uncle Tony. But you better bring two treats next time. You owe us.'

Tony snorted. He'd suspected he wasn't going to get off lightly.

'Have you seen a newborn lamb before, Mel?'

'Have you seen one being born?'

'It's really gross.'

Mel looked over her shoulder at Tony, her eyebrows drawn up in a 'what have you got me into' expression.

Tony gave her the thumbs-up and climbed out of the cab. Heading into the house he heard Jody clattering around out back.

'Jodes?'

'In the usual spot,' she called out.

The kitchen. The place they'd spent so much of their youth mooching about while their father worked all hours in the pub. It was the place Tony had learned how to do cryptic crosswords, his grandfather patiently explaining the many rules and tricks over and over again while Jody tried to perfect their grandmother's pikelets. They'd done their homework there, or at least pretended to... they'd moaned about teachers and fellow students only to be told that if they didn't have anything nice to say they shouldn't say anything at all... and they'd learned how to grow into upstanding adults. The day their grandmother had died, a piece of Jody's and Tony's hearts had withered. As had their grandfather's. So much so that he'd passed not long after, leaving them alone with their work-obsessed father. A man who had chosen to channel his grief for the passing of his wife into his work, rather than channelling it into loving his children.

The rustic room hadn't changed over the years. Bare wooden floorboards in need of a good polish. A formica table with chrome legs sat in the corner, turquoise-coloured vinyl seats surrounding it. Wooden doors hung open revealing shelves bulging with preserves. And the potbelly stove in the corner roared away, keeping the room toasty warm.

'What's she doing here?' Jody nodded to Mel, who was being dragged out to the lower field to meet the latest additions to the small farm.

'Mel? She's here to meet some animals. And some sheep.'

'Don't call my boys animals.' She flicked the damp tea towel she was using to dry dishes in his direction.

'How about I call them delinquents? Would that make you happy?'

Jody stuck her tongue out.

'Well, I can see where they get their rough streak from.'

'Funny, dear brother, super funny. Why don't you start your own comedy night at the pub? You could be the star of the show. You'd make... well, you'd have to pay people to stay... so... yeah...'

'Who's the comedian now?' Tony sat himself in a chair and grabbed an apple from the fruit bowl.

'But really, why's she here?'

'She's been having a rough time. Her mother's come to stay.'

'And she's not happy about that?' Jody's eyebrow arched in surprise. Tony knew exactly what she was thinking. It was exactly what he'd thought. Who wouldn't want to have their mother around? It was one of the things they'd wished for most in their lives.

Tony rubbed the apple on his jumper. 'To be fair to Mel, you haven't met her mother.'

'So, not the kind and loving, cuddly, homely type?'

'More like the uber-cougar. Even I'm afraid of her.'

'Well, you'd be prime meat, wouldn't you?' Jody put down the tea towel and sat at the table opposite where he'd plonked himself down.

'No. Not when I'm engaged to marry her daughter.'

Tony tried not to smirk as Jody's face went as ashen as the light layer of fire dust that had settled on the hearth.

'Engaged?'

'Yup.' He took a bite of the apple, chewed and swallowed, distracting himself from laughing.

'You?'

'Aha.' He nodded, mashing his lips together as they threatened to give the game up by twitching.

'Do I need to call a doctor?' She leant forward and laid her damp palm on his forehead.

'Nup. I'm marrying Mel. At least, that's what her mother thinks.'

'You rotter! You had me going for a second there.' Jody punched his arm, making him laugh.

'You punch like a girl.'

'Want me to try again?'

He shook his head. Jody punched every bit as hard as any bloke. The dull ache in his bicep was proof enough of that.

'So why are you in a fake engagement?'

'That damn coffee machine's to blame. Actually, no, the pub's to blame. She's helping me revamp the menu, teaching me how to cook proper food, and all I have to do is pretend to be engaged to her while her mother's here for the next few days.'

The image of the towering pile of luggage flitted into the front of his mind, sending a shiver of unease through his body. 'Well, I hope it's just for a few days…'

'But why does she need you to be her fiancé?'

Tony shrugged his shoulders. He still had no idea what the deal was. There hadn't been time to talk about it.

'You mean you're having to fake-like a woman, love her even, and you don't even know why?' Jody shook her head, her eyebrows arrowed together in confusion. 'I'm sorry, that's mental. Crazy. I had no idea Mel was nuts… she seemed so sane, so together.'

'She's not nuts. She's actually kind of amazing…'

Jody's eyes brightened. Damn it. He should've kept his mouth shut.

'So you like her then?'

He could almost see Jody putting on her detective cap.

'Of course I like her, she's a nice girl.'

'You know that's not what I mean. Has my brother finally met his match? Do I see that bachelor hat of yours being hung up?'

Tony rolled his eyes at his sister's ridiculous question. 'Never. Not going to happen. But a man's gotta do what a man's gotta do, and right now this man has got to figure out a way to keep The Bullion going.'

'I've said it before…'

'Closing those doors or selling up is not an option. That's my home.' And he had a promise to keep. A promise he'd never told Jody about, not wanting her to worry about the pub when she had two little ones to care for all on her own.

'And this isn't?' Jody looked around the farmhouse kitchen.

'This place is your home now. Yours and the boys. The Bullion's mine.'

Jody nodded her acceptance. She knew how much that place meant to him even if she didn't know why.

'How bad are things, Tony? At The Bullion? I've heard the rumours. Mrs Har…'

'Mrs Harper needs to stop gossiping or she'll never be allowed to set foot in The Bullion again.'

'So you'd ban one of your few remaining customers and get yourself into even more financial trouble? Mrs Harper may be a shocking gossip, but her sources are rarely wrong. I heard a debt collector was sniffing around.'

Tony crossed his arms over his chest, tipped his head back and stared at the smoke-mottled ceiling. 'I could never understand why Dad wouldn't show me the books. He said everything was okay, despite the downturn in customers. Turned out that was his pride talking.'

'Like father, like son,' Jody observed.

'What's that supposed to mean?' Tony glared at his sister.

Jody shrugged. 'Well, you could have come to me – not that I've any money. We could get a mortgage on this place, though, free up some cash…'

'McArthurs don't do mortgages. You know that. We buy outright or we don't buy at all.'

'McArthurs also don't get into such massive debts that we're in danger of losing everything. Come on, Tony. Surely we can blow off those old family rules for The Bullion. We don't have to live in the past, follow the past rules, not like Dad did.'

'No. I won't let you do it. How would you pay off the mortgage? I don't see any rich folk begging for you to sculpt them something. And the farm only makes enough for you to get by as it is.'

'I'd find a way. Tony, you've done so much for me and the boys. Let me do this for you.'

Tony shook his head. 'Not going to happen. Besides, Mel's teaching me how to make cottage pie tonight, and apparently lamb shanks once I get some in. I'll be fine.'

'As I said before… like father, like son.' Jody folded the tea towel and placed it over the oven rail. 'Hmmmm, I'm surprised the boys haven't come in yet. We should make sure they haven't started flinging sheep poo at your guest. I mean, fiancée.'

Tony and Jody wandered out to the backyard to see the kids and Mel leaping about the field, all three of them giggling helplessly as the lambs bleated and jumped along with them.

Mel's face was filled with joy as she kicked her legs up in the air, her hair flopping over her face, enough to hide her eyes, but not that smile. Warm, rich. Inviting.

Something twitched downstairs.

Down, boy. Now is neither the time nor the place. In fact, when it came to Mel, he didn't think it ever would be. She might be amazing, but he'd never do her justice. She needed someone who'd stick around for the long haul.

Mel glanced up at that second and waved.

'Uncle Tony!' the boys called in glee. 'Come jump with us.'

'I'll leave you boys and that crazy friend of mine to your jumping, I'm happy to watch.'

'Killjoy!' Mel yelled, resuming her mad leaping, her slim body taking to the air with grace, unlike the wobbly-legged lambs who looked like their little legs were about to collapse under their weight.

He turned back towards the house, shaking his head

in amusement when he heard a very Mel-like voice *baa* in his direction.

If only she were a one-night kind of girl.

***

'So, I hear you're to be marrying my brother.' Jody fixed Mel with a suspicious eye as she stirred sugar into their tea.

Oh God. So Tony had told Jody and now Jody was giving her the wickedest hairy eyeball in the history of the world.

A flash of heat ran through Mel's body, hitting her cheeks. She placed her hands, cold from the brisk, wintry air, onto them to cool them down.

'I am. But not really. You do know that, don't you?'

'Of course she does.' Tony gave Mel's shoulder a reassuring rub. 'Jody, leave Mel alone.'

'I'm sorry, but I'm just being protective of you, Tony. Trouble never seems that far away.'

'When have I ever been in trouble?'

'Well there was Linda. And Amber. And Cherrilyn. They were pretty riled up after you broke things off with them.'

Mel's mouth dropped. Tony's bed-hopping had left a trail of broken hearts? She knew of his reputation, but she'd never heard about any of that. No wonder she didn't want to get involved with him. She liked her heart rock solid.

Tony waved Jody's accusations away. 'Those three girls didn't know the meaning of the word "fun". Besides, I haven't had any ranty women on my doorstep in ages. That all happened when I was in my late teens and had yet to learn the art of explaining once was enough.'

Once was enough. Yeah, that summed up Tony. Although at least he was honest about it – these days, anyway. At least he didn't make promises he couldn't keep, unlike her mother.

'So what's the deal, Mel?' Jody passed her the steaming cup of tea and sat at the table. 'Why does your mother coming here mean you have to be engaged all of a sudden?'

Mel's stomach tightened. She'd hoped she wouldn't have to go into this in depth with Tony, let alone his sister.

'Yeah, I'd be keen to know that, too, Mel. A guy needs a bit of backstory if he's going to forego seeing psychotic women in order to be a fake future-husband for a couple of days. Am I going to have to get out the cattle prod?' Tony teased.

'Erm. I'd prefer you didn't.' She took a sip of her tea.

'Then, spill. What's up with you and your mum? Don't tell me she's intent on your settling down and making babies so the only way you were going to shut her up was to have a fiancé while she stayed. Because there's a hole in that story – you'd eventually have to produce babies and there is no way in the world I'm helping you with that.'

'Well, it's sort of like that.' Mel slapped her hand over her eyes, not wanting Tony and Jody to see how embarrassed she was. Faking a fiancé had seemed such a good idea at the time. And Tony had been right there. He needed her cooking knowledge. She needed a man. Deal done. But now? 'God, this is turning into such a mess.'

'What? What do you mean, "mess"?' Tony's teasing turned to suspicion.

Mel wondered if she could outrun him and a cattle prod.

'The thing is, my mother has commitment issues. Over-commitment issues. She believes in love and marriage so much she's done it four times. Maybe five? Six? I don't know. I've lost count.'

'So you've got to get married, too?' Tony leant back in his chair, his brow furrowed in confusion. 'Isn't that a bit…'

'Stupid?' Jody jumped in.

'Yep.' Mel agreed. 'Very. But if she came here and I wasn't happily settled down she'd do what she's always done and that'd be take me out to hunt for a man for her as well as for myself. It's humiliating.' Though not as humiliating as being dumped on her grandmother's doorstep as a child every time her mother met a new man and needed to wrangle him into giving her a ring.

'But asking my brother to marry you wasn't?'

Mel rubbed her eyes and slumped back in the chair.

77

'That would be called desperation. It was a dumb idea. We all know Tony's not the marrying type and now Valerie's talking about putting an engagement notice in the local paper, even though I begged her not to... the village is going to freak.'

'Hold on? What?' Tony jumped up and started pacing the room. A small vein in his temple popped out. Mel was pretty sure she could even see it pulsing. 'I'd kind of hoped to keep this under wraps as much as possible. Easy in. Easy out. And now everyone is going to know about it? How are we going to get ourselves out of this mess?'

'Oh, Tony, I'm so sorry. You've no idea. I shouldn't have asked you. I shouldn't have dragged you into it. I was just... like I said... desperate.'

'Desperate?' Tony spat the word out. 'Nuts more like it. Well, we'll just have to break up. Tell her it's over before the paper goes out. Say things have been rocky for a while and that we've realised we're not meant to be together.'

'No, Tony, don't. Please,' Mel begged, the images of the men her mother was attracted to flickering through her mind.

'Why? It's not a big deal. It happens all the time.'

But it was a big deal. Mel couldn't handle another hunting mission with her mother. And those horrible men. All so wrong. Slimy, handsy leeches. Not that her mother cared. She adored the attention, would take it from anyone, anywhere. No matter the consequences, to her or to her daughter.

'Look, Tony, I'm sorry. It just is what it is and you can't back out because we've got our deal. I help you revamp the pub's menu so you can revive The Bullion, and you help me survive my mother's visit. You can't renege. You promised.'

'Sounds like Tony's getting the raw end of the deal.' Jody's arms were crossed, her legs, too. Disapproval radiated off her.

'He is. He wasn't meant to…' Mel trailed off. It had been a long time since she'd felt this helpless, and once again her mother was the cause of it. 'I'll make this up to you, Tony. I'll create the best damn menu this village has ever seen. This district. You'll have the glitterati from London coming down to try it.'

'You'd better, Mel.' Tony stopped his pacing and turned to her. His body tight and tense. His sister's look of disapproval mirrored in his own face, but even more so. 'You'd bloody better.'

***

The ride home had been in silence. Not a word said. Tony had seen Mel shoot apologetic looks in his direction, but he'd ignored them, pretended not to see them. He was in no mood for playing nice.

'Stop looking at me with those big brown eyes of yours.'

The seat's leather crackled as Mel squirmed in her seat. 'Well, we can hardly sit in silence the whole way back.'

'We can. I have no problem with silence.'

'But, Tony...'

'But Tony what?' His knuckles turned white on the steering wheel as his irritation surged. '"But Tony", we need to sort something out? "But Tony", it's only for a few weeks. "But Tony", you agreed to do this, so it's not like it's my fault?'

That was the crux of it right there. What annoyed him the most. In a way this whole damn situation had been of his own making. If he hadn't been so stuck in his ways, determined to keep The Bullion the same as the day his dad had died, so determined to live up to the vow he'd made to his father... Hell, if he'd been able to convince his father to move with the times, look outside his own little world to see what others were doing, he wouldn't be in this predicament.

Mel shot him a cautious look. 'I know you won't like me saying it, but I am sorry. I did plead with her. All but got down on my knees but she didn't listen. She never does. It's why I was so emotional earlier. That, and I was afraid of how angry you'd be when I told you.'

Tony kept his eyes on the road, knowing one glance at a dejected-looking Mel would soften him. Make him go easy on her.

'God, every time I see her I hope she's changed. Become

more caring, more settled, more like a proper mother. But she's still the same old Valerie. Twister of words, manipulator of situations.'

Mel sounded so tortured, so wounded. What had her mother done to her? Tony had a feeling it was a hell of a lot more than just trawling for men in bars.

'I'll call the paper and see if they'll pull it.' Mel's words were soft but determined, like the beaten soldier who refuses to give up.

Tony softened. *Damn it*. She'd crept under his skin. He didn't need to see her looking dejected to know that she was. It danced upon every word coming out of her cute little mouth.

'Can't have been easy growing up with a mum like yours, from what I can figure anyway.'

'You have no idea.' Mel's voice wobbled.

Tony pulled over to the side of the road.

'What are you doing?' Mel wiped away a tear. 'We've got to get back to town. The pub's due to open, and you still need to learn how to cook something...'

'Just shut up for a second,' Tony implored. Scooting over the truck's worn and cracked leather seats he wrapped his arms around Mel and brought her close. Her body hardened in resistance, but he refused to let go and began to stroke her back in a gentle rhythm until she gradually relaxed, then melted into him. A patch of moisture grew on his shirt as she released whatever it was she'd been going through. Pressure from the past day or two? Or her whole life? It seemed Mel hadn't had it all that easy. No wonder she hid under a veneer of pink-and-green café and bright, stripy-coloured hair. It was her armour. Bold enough to stop people looking too deeply. Bright enough to keep them at arm's length. The vet hadn't stood a chance with a person like Mel, someone who by all appearances was easy going and nice, an uncomplicated woman to date, but who, once you scratched the surface, was tough, determined and, whether she knew it or not, every bit as complicated as her mother. Though, he suspected, not on purpose, and not in a way that meant she wanted to hurt anyone. She was only determined not to hurt herself.

Yet here she was, marshmallow-soft in his arms, trusting him with a little piece of her heart. A sliver of her soul.

The weight of the realisation sat heavily in the pit of Tony's stomach. He'd never let a woman get this close before. Especially one he respected and liked. He sucked in the fresh country air, grateful for the broken window that refused to wind all the way up. His whole adult life, the only thing he'd cared about, made an effort with, was The Bullion and maintaining the life's work of his father. And the memory of his mother. To him The Bullion was more than a business; it was the last standing relic of his family and he was going to do everything he could to keep it going, even if it meant being lumbered with a fiancée for God knew how long.

The soft hitches against his shirt had stopped, Mel's breathing had slowed. He brushed away a lock of black hair. Her eyes had closed. Long, black lashes settled peacefully on tear-stained cheeks. She was asleep. And it looked like he wasn't going anywhere.

CHAPTER FIVE

'So you and Tony are a thing, hey?' The girl with the curly black hair, a relatively new customer, tipped Mel a knowing wink. 'That was quite some announcement in the paper.'

Mel nodded and focused on heating the milk, not wanting the customer to see the guilt in her eyes. She'd tried to stop the paper printing the news but, by the time they'd returned home from Jody's, it had been too late. The paper was out, the locals had come in and offered congratulations, and only Mrs Harper had thought to query their relationship, which was fully understandable. It wasn't like Tony and herself were in full-on flirt mode. The opposite. Since they'd arrived back from his sister's house he'd been distant. Distracted. Her show of emotion wouldn't have helped. Probably made him think she was a total psycho. Heck, she had been a total psycho. Had been? *Was*, more like it. Who forced a man to be her fiancé in order to keep a crazy mother off their back? Especially when that man would do anything to keep his business afloat.

'Earth to Mel? Are you in there?' The girl waved her hand in front of Mel's eyes, gold bracelets jangling and flashing.

'Sorry, I'm in here, there. I'm...yes.' Mel swept a hand over her tired eyes and refocused on heating milk.

'The town can't quite believe it, you know?'

Mel blinked, confused. Believe what? And what was the name of the customer again? Hope? Joy? Something uplifting.

'Tony was such a loner, even at school. I never thought he'd let anyone that close. Apart from Jodes, that is.'

Mel poured the milk into the crema, happy to let her customer blather on. Who knew what she might learn about Tony? Seemingly super-relaxed on the outside but a whole lot more complicated in the middle? She was starting to get that all right.

'Even when his mother passed away he soldiered on. Just like his dad, really. Chip off the old block and all that.'

'Here's your cappuccino.'

The chatterbox stopped yakking for a second and took a sip.

'Mmmm, so good. Your café is saving my life, you know. It's the one bit of sanity in this crazy village.'

'Thank you...' Mel scrambled to find the name. Usually she had no trouble with names or faces, but dealing with Tony, her mother, and sleeping on her back-breaking couch had left her exhausted.

'Serena.'

'Serena. I'll remember that.'

'You might. I've only told you four times already.' With a flash of a smile she spun round and flounced out of Mel's in a shock of hot-pink top and neon-orange skirt.

'Well, it's good to see someone in this town isn't afraid to play with fashion. I mean, really, Mel, would it kill you to put on a skirt and wear a dash of lippy?'

Mel closed her eyes and inhaled deeply, determined not to let her mother's nit-picking get to her. She glanced up at the clock. It had just gone eleven. Strange. While never one for getting up at the crack of dawn, Mel had never known her mum to sleep in this late on a regular basis. Was something up?

Dumb question. Something was definitely up. Her mother had been here for over forty-eight hours now and, apart from that first night when she'd turned up at the pub, she'd yet to make Mel take her on a man-pulling trawl, let alone ask her where the men liked to hang out, which would only be at The Bullion anyway. Instead, she'd hung out at the apartment, driving Mel mental with questions about how Tony and she had met, when they were getting married, what dress she was going to wear, and would she be dying her hair a 'normal' colour so she wouldn't look at the photos thirty years from now and regret how she'd styled herself.

If the badgering continued, Mel would take to drinking

the cooking sherry first thing. Or maybe commit spatula-cide.

'Hi, Mum. Sleep well?'

'Like a dream. That bed of yours is divine and, oh, it's nice not having to share it with anyone. Although, I do miss having someone to snuggle up to in the small, cold hours of the night.'

The little hairs on the back of Mel's neck stood to attention, sending a shiver down her spine. 'So what happened to...' Mel tried to come up with the name of her mother's latest paramour and failed. There'd been so many she'd given up trying to keep track of them all.

'Donald? We're done. I found him in some bar kissing some other woman up against a billiards table.'

I see your taste in men hasn't improved. Mel bit back the retort. Experience and a fair few tongue-lashings had taught her not to question her mother's choice in men. It was as if her mother didn't want to admit she would take anything, anyone. Perhaps because, if she did, the dating pool would suddenly get a whole lot smaller.

'So that's why you're here? Not to spend time with me but to find yourself another man? Good luck with that. Rabbits Leap isn't exactly known for being a source of singletons.'

'I know. I've one of those dating apps on my mobile and there was no one to swipe. But still, you never know what you'll find. Or who you'll find if you look closely enough. I mean, look at you. You found Tony. Even with that crazy hair and lack of fashion sense. There may be hope for me yet. Besides, I don't need an app. I have you, and I'm sure after a year here you must know a single man or two who could entertain me.'

Mel gritted her teeth and picked up the tongs to rearrange the scones in the cabinet. Why couldn't she be enough for her mother? Why was she only seen as a means to an end?

'Oh, and you don't have to sleep over with me either, you know. I'm a grown woman. I can look after myself. Go sleep with the love of your life tonight. Besides, if I do find someone here in this little spot of yours I wouldn't want them having to see you asleep on the couch on our way to the bedroom. Total passion killer.'

Mel began to shake her head. There was no way she was sleeping with Tony. And there was doubly no way her mother was bringing a man home to *her* flat, to sleep with in *her* bed.

'No, no.' Valerie held up her hand, stopping the non-verbal protest in its tracks. 'You need to spend time with your beloved. Also, I need to get to know him better if he's to be my son.' Valerie's claw-like fingernails tapped rhythmically on the counter. 'Though, to be honest, I'd hoped he'd be something else when I first saw him. He's positively dreamy, Melanie.'

Mel fought the urge to take the tongs and use them to

squeeze her mother's lips shut. 'I don't know that there's time for any get-togethers while you're here, Mum. I have to work here and Tony's probably got pub business to attend to.'

'Well, if the days are out, what about dinner?'

'He'll be working. I'll no doubt be roped into helping him.'

Mel didn't think she'd be roped in at all. Not with Tony acting like he'd rather sleep in a snake pit than come close to her, but the last thing she wanted was Valerie snooping around Tony, asking questions, finding out the truth and leaving Mel in the embarrassing situation of having to explain why she'd lied, and then being back to square one. Wing-woman for her man-hungry mother.

'Well, how about we all help him? I've worked in bars before. Remember? When we lived in Thornton for that year.'

Mel cringed. She remembered that *annus horribilis* all right – it was one of many her mother had inflicted upon her in her quest to find the love of her life, or at least the love that'd do for now. But unlike the others, it was the year she realised her mother was never going to make Mel her priority.

'It'll give me a chance to scope out the gents of the area, too.' Valerie nodded to herself then zeroed in on Mel, as if daring her to say no. 'So that's settled. Text Tony and let him know he's getting the Sullivan treatment. Lucky boy doesn't know what's about to hit him.'

'Pint of lager coming up!'

Tony watched Mel's mum work the crowd as he mashed potatoes to put on top of the cottage pie mixture he'd made earlier that evening. She was all smiles and hair-flicking and little laughs. The few locals that had remained loyal to The Bullion loved her. She had a natural knack with people, an ability to take a grumpy-looking customer and make him giggle like a schoolgirl with a bit of gentle teasing. Even the rugby players who'd started downing pints the moment the bar opened at three, becoming rowdier and more raucous as the hours went by, laid off the booze when she'd given them a stern warning that they'd be out on their ear if they didn't calm down. She'd even convinced them to buy the steak special for dinner in order to soak up the booze. Valerie was good for business. Hell, if he wasn't stuck in this insane charade with Mel he'd have offered her a job.

'Are you okay there, my soon-to-be son-in-law? Need me to get you anything? A lemonade? Beer? Whisky on the rocks? I would say "me" but we both know how inappropriate that would be.'

'Mother.' Mel's hands flew to her hips. 'Really?'

Tony cringed. Of all the times for Mel to come out of the kitchen.

'I've been biting my tongue since you got here. But

honestly, out of all the men you could hit on you had to hit on the one who's taken? By your daughter? Will you ever change?'

'I was just teasing him, honey. Promise. Making sure he wasn't one of those dirty-dog types.'

'We don't all have your tastes, Mother.'

Uh-oh. Fight club. Even the boozers sensed it, their loud chatter and guffaws calmed to pin-dropping quiet speculation, and the odd snort of laughter.

'Mel…' Valerie placed her hands on the bar as if to steady herself. 'This isn't the time or the place for this conversation.'

'The thing with you, Mother, is it never is, but I'm tired of spending my life afraid…'

'Woah.' Tony spun round to face Mel and raised his eyebrows at her, reminding her of the captive audience. Another half spin and he was refereeing the two of them. 'Ladies, I'm sure if these good people had wanted to watch a drama unfold they'd have stayed home and flicked on the television. But they're here to drink and eat and have a good time. Am I right, people?'

Mutterings of 'spoilsport' and murmurings of 'I was enjoying that' met his ears. Damn.

'Next round is on the house!'

In a second the surly glowers of the patrons had switched over to whoops of joy and hollers of happiness.

Mel grabbed him by his sleeve and pulled him close.

'You can't afford to do that. You had to beg the butcher to let you put the steaks on tick.'

'Well, I couldn't afford to have you two go at it like a couple of alley cats either. I don't know what's gone on with you two, but your mother was right, this is not the place to have it out.'

'Well, thanks for the support, Tony. I really appreciate it. And what are you doing mashing the potatoes at the bar? That's not hygienic!' Mel snarled and took off back to the kitchen.

Tony rubbed the back of his neck. When had his life become so difficult?

'Don't worry about my daughter, Tony. She'll be back to her usual solid self tomorrow. She's never been one to hold a grudge, luckily for me.'

So Valerie was aware she'd caused Mel some issues? Good. But did she realise how deep-seated those issues were? He saw guilt flicker through those blue eyes. Yeah, she knew. But was she willing to do anything about it?

'All right, you lot, out you go. It's closing time and we've all got to get to bed.' Tony set the megaphone down and started cleaning down the bar.

'Noticed you didn't say "get to sleep", Tony?' One of his regulars gave him the thumbs-up. 'You and your soon-to-be-Mrs going to burn off a little extra energy?'

'You want to set foot back through these doors tomorrow?' Tony grinned as his customer turned and slunk out the door, throwing him another cheeky thumbs-up at the threshold, before disappearing into the night.

'Well, that was a long day.'

Mel appeared from out the back wiping her hands on a tea towel. Her hair was mussed, dark circles ringed her lower eyes, and there was a splodge of sauce on her cheek. She should've looked a mess but somehow she looked more attractive than ever.

'Here, give me that tea towel.' Before being offered it, Tony grabbed the towel with one hand and Mel's wrist with the other and pulled her close.

Mel gasped and made to pull back but relaxed when Tony raised the tea towel to her cheek.

'You didn't have to stay this long.' He dabbed at the red splodge and half wondered what she'd do if he'd licked it off instead.

Mel shrugged. 'I had to. You were snowed under and the kitchen was busy.'

'She wasn't going to hit on me again, not that she really was in the first place.'

Mel's gaze dropped to the floor. So he'd been right. She'd been keeping an eye on her mother.

'For the record, I'm not interested in her. She's just about old enough to be my mother.'

'Well, that hasn't stopped men your age before.'

'Well, I'm not one of those men.' He placed the tea towel on the bar. 'There, you're all clean.'

'Look, I need to apologise. I shouldn't have had a go at her in the pub. I'm sorry. I don't know what came over me. It's not like you and I are for real anyway.'

He hooked his finger under her chin and tilted her head up. Her eyes were bright, and there was that ever-present hint of sadness.

The corners of Mel's lips lifted in a half-smile. 'Thanks for sorting out the tomato sauce. I've been meaning to get to it all night.' The tip of her tongue darted out and flicked over her lips, leaving them glossy with moisture.

What would she taste like right now? After an evening spent sampling the food he'd made? Salty? Sweet? A mixture of both? Should he dare find out?

The kitchen door swung open and Valerie walked through, pulling a fresh keg along behind her. 'You two had best be staying with each other tonight, because it doesn't look like you can bear to be apart.'

Mel leapt away from Tony like a teenager caught in a romantic clinch by her parents. Or in this case, her parent. 'Mum, I can come home with you. Honestly, I don't want you up there all alone.'

'I'm not going to burn the place down, Mel. I've survived forty-six years without trashing a home, and I'm pretty sure I can go another night. Besides, you two clearly need some time together.'

The reality of the conversation hit Tony. Mel was going

to have to stay here, with him, in his room, since all the others were filled with snoring, snorting rugby players.

His heart began to hammer away in his chest. He breathed in, long and slow, hoping it would calm his jacked-up nerves. It was no big deal. No. Big. Deal. He'd had women stay over plenty of times. And it wasn't like he and Mel were going to have sex or anything. That was strictly off the table. Things around here did not need to get any messier. But what if this staying over became a regular thing? The hammering went into high gear, his blood pounding so hard in his ears he swore he could feel his eardrums vibrate.

'Valerie, Mel should stay with you. I'll have the rest of my life to spend with her but you two don't see each other all that often…'

Mel nodded. 'Exactly. What Tony said. We've seen each other maybe twice in five years? I'll come home with you. Let me get my coat and we'll get going.'

'Oh no you won't, Melanie.' Valerie settled the keg on the floor with a clunk. 'A good partnership means going to bed at night together. And besides, it's not like you want to spend time with me. Your behaviour earlier this evening proved as much.'

Mel squirmed under her mother's sharp gaze. 'Oh, Mother. I'm sorry I was short with you. I was busy, harried, and well, if I were to be honest, that couch isn't so comfortable to sleep on so I'm tired, too.'

Tony cringed as Mel gave her mother all the reasons she needed to further insist she sleep at his place.

'You're not sleeping well on the couch? Well then, you must stay with Tony.'

Mel paled and shifted from foot to foot, as if ready to run. 'No, honestly, the couch is fine, I'm just being a princess... Look, it really is easier for me to stay at the flat because I have to be up early...'

'Tony.' Valerie fixed Tony with an unwavering stare. 'Tell my daughter she's to do as her mother says.'

Tony raised his hands. 'Oh no, sorry, I don't tell your daughter to do anything she doesn't want to. She'd have my head.'

Mel smothered a grin with her hand, straightening her face when Valerie turned her attention back to her.

'Mel, if you try to come home with me I will lock you out.' Valerie darted past Mel and grabbed the café's keys out of Mel's coat.

'Mother, give me those back.' Mel reached for the keys but her mother dodged out of the way.

Tony watched the two women square off. Both as determined as each other. *Win, Mel, win.* There was no way her staying over was going to be a good idea. Despite his best intentions, the intimate moment they had shared just moments earlier played fresh in his mind. Who knew what could happen? Would happen? He didn't want to risk Mel's heart. Or their burgeoning friendship.

Mel took a step towards her mother. 'It's my café, Mother. Those are my keys.'

Valerie ducked out of Mel's reach as she made a grab for the keys. 'That may be so but I'm your guest and as your guest I'd like to be left alone, and it's not like you don't have another place to stay.'

Mel reached up and rubbed her eyes, then turned her gaze on Tony and mouthed, 'I tried, sorry.'

She had tried, but Mel was no match for her mother. Tony suspected no one was.

'Well, I can see you've come to your senses.' Valerie's face lit up in satisfaction. 'One more thing, Mel. Can I borrow your car?'

Mel's forehead crinkled. 'At this time of night? What for?'

'There's some tipsy patrons sitting outside, I'm going to drop them home. They're going to pay me. I might just have to stick around and start a little shuttle service. It looks like this town could do with one.'

Mel's face further paled as she nodded her assent.

Tony wondered if his face matched hers? Was Valerie serious about starting a business in Rabbits Leap? If she was, that meant she wasn't going anywhere. Soon. Ever. So much for things not needing to be any messier.

***

'So, this is awkward…' Tony leant against the wall beside his bed and waggled his eyebrows up and down.

Mel appreciated that he was trying to make light of the situation, but there was nothing light about it. A dense sense of doom filled every cell in her body. Valerie was talking about sticking around. She'd never done that before. She was incapable of it; she moved all the time. New towns, new friends, new men…

And there it was. A ray of hope.

'Don't worry, Tony. Mum won't be here long. She'll get bored. There's no men to entertain her in Rabbits Leap.'

'I wasn't talking about your mother. I was talking about this.' He indicated to himself, her and the bed. A small double, with a very definite dip in the middle.

'How old is that thing?' Mel screwed up her nose. She needed a good sleep and it didn't look like the bed would provide it, especially since she was to be sharing it with a tall, broad man who'd easily take up two thirds of it.

'About nine months older than me.'

'You sleep on the bed you were conceived on? I'm sorry, but that's just…' She shivered in horror.

'Well it's not like I've had the money to replace the beds. And besides, people buy second-hand beds all the time and you can't tell me they're not buying beds that people have been conceived in, or died in for that matter. Oh, and don't worry, before you get any ideas, my mother was kind enough to pass away in a hospital bed and Dad on the floor down in the pub.' He folded his arms across his broad chest. 'Mum was cancer, Dad was a heart attack, in case you were wondering about that as well.'

Horror flooded through Mel. 'Oh no. God. Sorry. I didn't mean to bring up painful memories… and I wasn't even thinking about that. But, um, yeah, thanks for telling me…' She looked down at her feet and tried to stem the curiosity that had been building since Tony first mentioned his mother's passing. 'You know, you don't talk about your mum much and, um, I've noticed there's not really any hint of her about the place… I mean, well, you know I never had a father, not a real one. So I know it can be hard not to have a parent around. I understand that it can be tough…'

'I survived. Besides, I had Jody, and when Dad wasn't working he would take me out to the lake for a spot of fishing.'

'How often did he do that?' Mel leaned against the doorjamb, glad to take a little weight off her aching feet.

'Twice a year. Christmas Day and Good Friday. Only days the pub ever closed.' Hurt flickered through his eyes.

'That must've been hard. Sounds like you pretty much raised yourselves.'

'We had my grandparents. That farm where Jody and the boys live? That was theirs. They passed it on to us.'

'And not your dad?'

'Dad was never a farmer. It was too lonely for him. He

liked people. He liked to have a laugh, a drink. Granddad reckoned the moment he laid eyes on this building when he was a youngster he decided he'd own it one day. Saved up every cent he ever got, took on three jobs and then one day came in and made a cash payment. An offer the owner couldn't refuse. After that day he barely left the place.'

'And your mum was okay with that?'

Tony shrugged.

Did he not know his mother at all? Did he not care?

'So, why did you take over the pub? You could've gone to the farm, too, right?'

'I'm not much of a farmer either.'

'Like father, like son?'

'Something like that…' Tony mashed his lips together and looked away.

'So how'd your dad react when your mum died?' Mel had a feeling she knew the answer, but she wanted to hear it from Tony.

Another shrug. 'Took all her pictures down, packed away all her stuff. Worked harder. Longer hours. More socialising.'

'He was heartbroken.'

Tony sucked in his bottom lip and released it. 'I guess so. Never said anything much to me about that. Never spoke about Mum again, to be honest. It was like saying her name would make the pain worse.'

Mel's heart went out to Tony. He would've grown

up having to keep his emotions on lockdown. Probably figured the only way to get his dad's respect, attention and love was to love the pub as much as he did. That nothing else, no one else, was worth his time. Did Tony realise his life had been shaped by that event and his father's reaction to it? Mel pondered asking him, but one look at his hunched shoulders and the corded muscles straining at his neck and she thought better of it.

'So, what are we going to do about this?' She walked over to the bed and sank onto it, cringing as it squeaked under her weight. Did she just hear a spring ping?

'I could sleep on the floor,' Tony offered. 'There's a spare blanket and pillow in the wardrobe.'

'No, don't, please.' Mel tried to jump up in protest but failed, the mattress refusing to release her from its pillowy grip. 'I can. I will. This is your bedroom and I got us into this.'

'Well, I agreed to the whole plan, and besides, if I hadn't bought that coffee machine none of this would've happened.'

'So we're both to blame?'

Tony grinned, his shoulders inched down. 'Something like that.'

'So we should both sleep on the ground?'

'Or both sleep in the bed.'

A vision of the two of them tangled together popped into Mel's mind. Her soft curves against his hard chest.

Their lips within kissing distance. Hands within touching distance. What would his hands feel like on her body? Soft and tender? Hard and demanding? Desire pooled hot and heavy in her lower stomach. It was tempting. So tempting. Too tempting. And entirely inappropriate.

'Shall we sleep top 'n' tail style? So, you know, you won't try and get all amorous on me?'

'Me?' Tony scoffed. 'Get all amorous? Never. Well, not if you don't want me to…'

The invitation lingered in the air. Its promising tendrils wrapping themselves around the sensible corners of Mel's mind, suffocating them. How easy it would be right now to haul herself up off the bed, march over to Tony, pull off that tight, white T-shirt, run her hands over his chest, that stomach, up into his hair. To lower his face to hers, breathing in that heady malty scent, before finding those lips…

'I don't know if that would be a good idea.' She bit her lip, cursing her sensible mind. A night of passion was being presented to her. A night of pleasure. Good, old-fashioned, no-strings-attached fun. And she was turning it down. Was she nuts? No. Not nuts. She was just her. Boring old sensible Mel, afraid to do anything a little wild, a little crazy, for fear she'd turn into the person that raised her. But really, what was the worst that could happen?

You have too good a time.

You fall for him.

He doesn't fall for you.

Things go bad.

You have to pack up and leave.

Another home.

Again.

Dumb, sensible brain. It had a point.

'Mel? You're a million miles away. Come back to me?'

The words were close, hovering over her head. That hoppy aroma filled her senses. Small rooms made for few steps.

She laid her hand on his chest. A barrier. A gentle 'no'.

Tony gazed down at her with curiosity. As if trying to figure her out. There was no anger there, though, despite the rejection. Only good humour. So that was it. He was just trying it on. What else should she have expected from Tony McArthur? That was who he was, what he did. Played it loose, kept it easy. Only committing to the rotting heap that was his father's poor excuse for a love life after his wife had died.

'It's been a long day, Tony.' She faked a yawn.

'It has.'

'I need sleep.'

He sighed. 'We both do.'

'So let's just both do that, shall we?'

'Sure.'

He turned from her and whipped his T-shirt off, revealing a disturbingly toned back. Mel stared, transfixed, at his rippling muscles as he tossed the scrap of material into a washing pile. He went to pull off his jeans. Oh, Lordy. *Look away. Look away.* But she couldn't. Not when that bubble butt of his had her hypnotised. There was the dull scrape of metal on metal as he undid his belt buckle. A swoosh as he pulled the belt out, followed by a thud as it landed on the wooden floor. She tried to swallow but her mouth was at a loss for moisture. Tony looped his thumbs over the top of the jeans and began to inch them down, revealing the top of what looked to be navy-blue underwear. The tight boxer type? An image of his strong thighs encased in the blue cotton, the same cotton that would house his...

'Can't you do that in the bathroom?' she squeaked, slapping her hands over her eyes. Thinking about what his underwear housed was not a good idea. It would only lead to an awkward morning conversation and an even more awkward rest of her life. That's if she didn't leave town due to the embarrassment of having thrown herself at Tony.

'I'm just showing you what you're missing out on. Giving you a chance to change your mind.' Was he teasing? It sounded like it. But she caught a hint of honesty in his words.

Mel spread her fingers a little to see Tony turn to her, a cheeky smirk lighting up his face, his cheekbones high in amusement. She dropped her gaze down, her breath hitched in her throat. He was naked, bar the underwear, and she was right. He was wearing tight, navy-blue boxers. And what they housed... even more impressive than she could've imagined. What with that action-seeking missile, the toned chest and perfectly formed six-pack, Tony was a sight to behold. But that's all he was going to be... a sight. And she wouldn't be holding anything.

'I'm not going to change my mind,' she said out loud, as much to herself as to Tony.

'And I don't sleep in pyjamas. Just my underwear. So you can either shuffle around this room blinded by your own hands or you can deal with it.'

'Infernal man.' She huffed, removing her hands to find no sign of Tony. Huh? Where'd he go? There was a dull slap of skin on cotton and the weight of the bed shifted underneath her.

She turned to see a grinning Tony, his head at the foot of the bed, his toes peeking out the blankets on the opposite side, top-and-tail style like she'd asked.

'You'd better not have stinky feet.'

'Never.'

'You'd better have a clean T-shirt.'

'What for?'

'I don't have any pyjamas.'

'You could sleep in your undies, too?'

Eyebrows raised in hope. A confident grin. A slow wink. The man was incorrigible and way, way too cute for his own good. Mel crossed then uncrossed her legs, trying to ignore the deep, low pulse in her body that was begging her to go to Tony, to satisfy her curiosity, her needs.

'They're in there.' He nodded to the chest of drawers by the bathroom door. 'Top drawer.'

'Thanks. Now put your head under the covers. I'm saving my body for my wedding night.'

'Pffft. Sure you are. More like you're saving your body for a bunch of scientists to dissect once you're dead.'

Mel laughed and swatted his head on the way past, glad of the dumb joke. A joke was friend territory, the absolute opposite of hot man in hot undies territory. She let out a long, quiet breath as she rummaged through the drawer, grateful for the moment to restore her equilibrium.

'So, have you ever had a night of fun, Mel? Ever just let loose and allowed your natural instinct to run free?'

The questions were muffled. His head was where it was meant to be. Good. Doubly good, because Mel didn't want him to see the flush that had crept over her face.

'Nope. Not once.'

'Were you a nun in a past life?'

'Probably.'

She saw a black cotton T-shirt and pulled it out. Size M. Good, it would cover her from neck to knees.

'What's the wildest thing you've ever done, Mel?'

What was with the questions? She whipped off her

jeans and sweater as fast as she could, then yanked on the T-shirt. Knee-skimming, just as she'd hoped.

'Are you going to leave a man suffocating under here or can I look now?'

'You can look.' She padded over to the bed and hopped in, pulled the blankets over her, then rolled promptly into the centre. Into Tony. His body radiated heat. Not the warm, comforting kind. Raw, animalistic heat, punctuated by that enticing scent of his.

Don't breathe, she willed herself, afraid of what could happen if she allowed that manly essence of his to intoxicate her.

'You haven't answered my question. What's the wildest thing you've done?'

Mel bunched a pillow up under her head so she could see Tony properly. 'Why do you even care?'

'I'm just interested. Think of yourself as a little mystery that I would like to solve. On the outside you look like you'd be up for a good time. Bright-pink streaks of hair and all that. But you're such a sensible Sally. Even your café is kind of like you. Bright and sparkly on the outside, but on the inside it's all cosy and warm and… old-fashioned.'

'Well, that's how you woo a girl, call her old-fashioned.' Mel rolled her eyes.

'Well, my regular style of wooing wasn't getting me anywhere.' He nudged her with his knee and gave her a good-natured smile. 'So is the hair your defence against the world?'

'What on earth are you on about, Tony?' Mel stiffened. He was getting a little too close for comfort.

'Your hair – is it like a form of armour? To stop people looking too hard. They see the harsh black, the bright pink, think 'tough chick' and leave it at that. When really, I suspect there's a great big baby-pink marshmallow underneath that bold hairdo of yours.'

'I don't have time for this.' Mel attempted to roll over onto her side but was promptly rolled back by the traitorous bed. 'My hair is my hair. I like pink and it contrasts well with the black.'

'I'm not so sure that's all there is to it...'

Mel's hands clenched into fists under the covers. Why couldn't Tony quit prying and leave her alone?

'I mean, look at what you wear. It's not just clothing, it's more of a uniform. Black jeans, sneakers and a long-sleeved top. Even in summer. Yet, the pinafore you wear in the kitchen and at the café is super-frilly and girly. I can't help but wonder what happened to you, Mel? What changed that girly girl into the unbending soldier?'

Mel gritted her teeth. How could she ever explain to Tony the years of fear and uncertainty she'd experienced. New towns. New homes. New men. A couple of them just as interested in her as they were in her mother. Her uniform, as he'd so rightly put it, had been a way of hiding. Not only her body, but also her soul. A way of hiding the person she feared she was, a person who wasn't good enough, wasn't likeable enough. Loveable enough. But she wasn't going to tell him that. He'd feel sorry for her and that was the last thing she wanted. It was time to go on the defensive.

'You ask me why I'm the way I am? Yet you hide here in this oversized shack day in day out? Dedicate yourself totally to something that will never love you back? That, if anything, is only causing you pain? Only a fool stays in a situation like that. That's not love. That's torture.' An errant tear slipped down her cheek. She could have been talking to herself.

Tony sat up, his expression frosty. 'Oversized shack? Don't you dare say a word against this place. You have no idea what she means to me, what she's meant to a lot of people.'

Mel swiped the tear away, not wanting Tony to see the effect his words were having on her, and struggled up onto her elbows. 'Stop calling her a "she". It's just a pub. A whole bunch of timber and tiles held together by a dozen rusty nails.'

'You don't get it, Mel. You never will. You're too busy living in your carefully constructed bubble to let others in, to see what they can bring to the table. You think The Bullion is nothing? Well, you're wrong. She's been a place of support, of joy, of mourning. She's lifted people up. She's brought people together. She's the heart of this town. Not the village hall down the way, not the grocery store, not your café. This place is what keeps Rabbits Leap together. And that's why I'll work my fingers to the bone to keep her going.'

'No, The Bullion *was* the heart of Rabbits Leap. Past tense. Maybe it was once the place where the villagers came together. But not any more. If it was, you wouldn't be in the trouble you're in. You wouldn't need me to help you bring it back to its past glory. But whatever, you keep deluding yourself about how great The Bullion is. How important it is.' Mel dropped back down onto the pillow. 'See where that gets you.'

'It'll get me a hell of a lot further than you. The people that do still come into The Bullion aren't just customers, they're friends. What about you, Mel? Have you managed to make a friend since moving here? Who pops in just to see how you are? Who cares about *you*?'

Mel closed her eyes. No one. That was the answer. Since moving here she'd set up her business and focused on that. Apart from the brief relationship with the vet she hadn't got close to a soul. Not that she'd let the vet in either. She didn't trust herself, didn't want him to get to know the real her, to discover the truth about her. The truth Tony had touched on.

What if Tony saw her for who she really was? Mel's stomach knotted up at the thought. All those years of hiding herself away and yet it felt like he could see through her iron-clad walls. What if she broke her own rule and told him everything? Would the closest thing she'd made to a real friend since she came to live in Rabbits Leap abandon her as well?

They lay in silence, skin touching, but a barrier between them, any hint of lust shattered into a million smithereens. Mel stared at the stained ceiling. Tony lay stiffly at her side. Not even his toes, perfectly formed, nicely trimmed and not at all stinky, wiggled at her.

'You don't have to stand on your own two feet all the time, Mel.' The words, sombre, honest, sincere, hung there, waiting for Mel to answer.

A ball formed in Mel's throat. That was the problem. She had to do exactly that, because unlike Tony, who had his sister and The Bullion's loyal customers, there was no one there to catch her if she fell.

Tony caught her hand and squeezed it. Maybe she was wrong, maybe she did have his support, but she didn't trust herself to find out.

CHAPTER SIX

So warm. So cosy. Mel snuggled down under the blankets. Just a few more minutes, then she'd get up and get going. Thank God she lived above the café; it made getting up a little late that much less of a...

She bolted upright. Well, tried to. The bed sucked her back into its snuggly embrace.

Stupid old broken bed.

She stretched out and grappled for her phone. 6.45? Surely it meant 4.45? She checked again. She'd overslept by two hours? That never happened. Even on her one day off she woke up at sparrow's fart. If she just hadn't had that ridiculous conversation with Tony last night this wouldn't have happened. She wouldn't have spent the night going over the past, wishing it had been different. Wondering if she could change, if she could allow herself to be the kind of person people popped in just to say 'hi' to, the way they did with Tony. If she'd just let things be, not risen to the bait, she'd have had enough sleep, barely, in order to get up and be ready to go at her usual time and her day would've run like clockwork.

Rocking back and forth, she managed to roll herself out of the bed, sucking in air as her feet hit the freezing wooden floorboards.

Where was Tony, anyway?

Mel shook her head. She didn't have time to be concerned about him. The café was due to open in less than fifteen minutes and she didn't have any scones, any muffins, any *anything* for her customers.

Yanking on yesterday's clothes she flew down the stairs, through the pub, shoved open the pub's door and stumbled into the morning gloom. The main street was quiet and she breathed a sigh of relief. No one about to witness her run of shame – not that she had anything to be ashamed about, which was probably a shame in itself. She sprinted the twenty odd metres to the café. And stopped.

The lights were on.

She'd turned them off. She knew she had. There was a routine. Lock door. Clear leftover food. Wipe tables. Refill salt and sugar and pepper shakers. Wash floors. Double-check the oven. And lastly, turn off the lights. Maybe her mother had turned them on? She swatted the idea way. Her mother wouldn't have turned the café lights on. She only had a key to the back door and the only light she might have needed to get her safely up the stairs was the kitchen light.

Had she been burgled? By a thief so intent on getting caught they'd let a local on an early walk see them stalking about stealing things? There was only one way to find out.

She turned the door handle and tugged at the door. It didn't budge. Good. She may have forgotten the lights, but at least she'd remembered to keep the shop safe. No burglars then.

She pulled the keys out of her pocket, then unlocked the door.

Ting-a-ling.

Mel jumped as the bell greeted her. Lack of sleep and the argument with Tony had made her edgy. Or should that be edgier? The last few days had felt like she'd been stalking over eggshells with winter-softened feet.

'There you are. Finally. What kind of business owner doesn't show up on time to her own business?'

Valerie's voice rang out from out back. She was in the kitchen? More to the point, she was up? At this hour?

Hold on, that wasn't the only weird thing. Fresh, golden, melted cheese-covered scones were piled up on the counter. What looked to be banana loaf was laid out on a tray. She sniffed the air. How had she not noticed the savoury aroma of sausage rolls cooking the moment she'd walked in?

'Mum?' she called out, cautiously. Maybe this was all a figment of her imagination? Maybe it was a dream? Or perhaps she really was losing her mind?

'Don't just stand out the front – come through. I'm not sure how you like your icing piped on the cupcakes...'

Cupcakes? Since when did her mother make cupcakes?

Mel lifted the hinged counter and headed into the kitchen.

'Tony?' What was he doing here?

Tony turned from the kitchen sink and gave her a soapy wave.

Okay, she had officially gone mad. This was all some insane hallucination. Oh well, she may as well go along for the ride and see where the dream ended up.

'Um, Tony, why are you doing the dishes?'

'I'm helping you out, what does it look like?' Tony turned back to the sink.

'But that makes no sense. You don't cook.'

'He does now. I had him make the scones. Didn't trust him with the cupcakes, though, so he's on dish duty,' Val interrupted. 'And quite frankly you need to buy a dishwasher. Doing it this old-fashioned way is ridiculous.'

'Luckily for your mum, I'm really good at doing dishes.' Tony waved a dripping brush in the air. 'Being a bachelor does have its uses.'

Oh hell. What had he just said? The B-word?

Dream-mother had stopped mixing the icing and was giving blabbermouth dream-Tony the hairy eyeball. The cat was out of the bag. Thank God this wasn't real or there'd be some serious explaining or backtracking to do.

'Bachelor?'

Dream-mother's suspicion was well and truly aroused. 'What do you mean "bachelor"?'

Turned out dream-mother was every bit as astute as her real-life mother.

'Oh. Um.' Dream-Tony squirmed under the sharpened gaze. 'It's just... well, I was single for so long before meeting Mel that I got used to fending for myself.'

'Oh, of course. That makes sense.' Dream-mother went back to mixing.

'What was the name of the soft toy I decided I was going to marry when I was seven?' Mel blurted the question out. Dream-mother wouldn't know the answer and she needed to make sure this was just a figment of her imagination, because it all looked a little too much like happy families to her.

'Mr Fluffybum. Why? I hope you're not still pining after him. I gave him away years ago'

Mel blinked. Okay, this was no dream. This was real. Tony and her mother were in her café's kitchen doing her job for her. What had come over them? Had someone set off some weird 'helpful' gas overnight?

'Would you stop staring at us like we've grown extra arms and heads please, Melanie.' Valerie pursed her lips as she began to spoon icing into the piping bag.

'Sorry, Mum, I just... I don't understand what's going on here? I slept in, which I never do. Ever. I ran here to find the both of you working away happy as kittens playing with a ball of wool. And everything looks fine. Nothing's burned. Nothing's broken.'

'My ego's a bit broken,' Tony pouted. 'When I woke your mum up and dragged her out of bed to help she called me all sorts of horrible names.'

'You woke her up? It was you who organised all of this? Why didn't you wake me up? Why'd you let me sleep in? I could have lost a day's takings.' Mel had half a mind to take the whisk out of her mum's hand and smear its chocolate-icing contents through Tony's hair. Was he still trying to ruin her business?

'I had to wake her up. I managed to follow that recipe of yours to make banana bread, but when I got to the cupcakes and all that folding business I knew I needed an extra pair of hands.'

'You should have woken me.' Mel turned her glare up to full force, as her exasperation began to build.

'You needed your sleep. You've been working way too hard. Burning the candle at both ends.'

'Melanie Sullivan, you stop being horrible to this man right here.' Valerie stopped beating the icing and jabbed the whisk in Mel's direction, spraying the kitchen floor and Mel in chocolatey droplets. 'Yes, I may have called him an ugly excuse for a male specimen when he pulled me out of a particularly nice dream involving one of those rugby players I saw at the pub the other night, but he is doing his best for you. How can you be angry at him for that?'

Mel paused. Her mother had a point. 'You're right. Tony, I apologise. But don't ever do it again. This business is all I have. I can't afford to have anything go wrong with it. You understand that, don't you?'

Tony nodded. 'Next time I'll wake you up.'

'Good.'

'Hold on.' Valerie plopped the whisk into the bowl. 'Your business is all you have? What are Tony and I? Chopped liver? I can't believe I raised such an ungrateful child.'

'Not ungrateful, Mother. Realistic. Prudent. Responsible.'

'You mean boring,' Valerie retorted.

Mel shrugged and smiled. She'd rather be boring than be her mother. Not that she was going to tell her that. The café was due to open and those cupcakes needed icing. 'Pipe the cupcakes in a simple swirl please, Mum. There's some gold dust in the cupboard, do be a dear and sprinkle it on top. You two seem to have it all under control, so I'm heading upstairs for a shower.'

Mel trudged up the stairs to the sounds of 'Slave Driver' and smiled. Her fake fiancé had saved her bacon. Her mother had grudgingly helped, which was better than not helping at all. Despite the minor tiff, they were all getting along. It was almost like having a proper family.

It was almost like all her secret hopes and dreams had come true. Mel clamped down on the bloom of happiness in her heart. It was almost like everything was too good to be true.

**

Mel set Tony's coffee and her hot chocolate down on the table and sat across from him, visibly glad to finally have the chance to take a break from work. 'So, what got you up so early?'

Tony tried not to smirk. As happy as Mel had looked leaving the kitchen earlier that morning, she'd come down after her shower with her eyes narrowed in suspicion and spent the better part of the day in interrogation mode. Why had he woken so early? Did her mother use cookbooks to make the food? Did her mother ask about their relationship? Had her mother tried to hit on him again? The questions had been endless.

'What got me up? A foot to the ribs,' he deadpanned. 'Your feet are bony.'

Truth be told, he'd not slept well. He'd faked sleep to ease the strain in the room but never dropped off, the argument he'd had with Mel turning over and over in his mind. He knew he'd hit a nerve. A nerve? More like the proverbial nail on the head. Mel refused to let people get close. She could say all the right things, be friendly, sweet, welcoming, but she had that hint of standoffishness, like she had checked out before you could. It didn't take a blind man to see it had something to do with her mother.

Now, Valerie, she was an interesting one, too. All maneater. No mum. Getting her out of bed in order to help her daughter had been a mission. Only the threat of pouring icy-cold water over her had finally dragged her out from under the duvet. It was like Valerie thought the world ought to revolve around Valerie. Everyone else was there to be used and tossed away when she was finished. Had she tossed her own daughter aside? Was that why Mel was so prickly?

'My feet are not bony. And I couldn't move in that rickety old bed of yours even if I did want to kick you. The thing had me trapped.'

'I've always found it easy to move in.' He winked and laughed as her cheeks blushed pink. Flirting with Mel was almost too easy.

'So are you going to tell me how you ended up in my café with my mother before the crack of dawn?'

'I wanted to help out a friend.'

'Who?' Mel's eyebrows lifted in surprise. 'Me?'

'Well, that's what you are, aren't you?'

'A hostage. That's what I am. Bound to this ridiculous deal of ours.' Mel took a sip of her drink and popped a marshmallow in her mouth.

'Is it hard to believe that I'd want to help you out after everything you've done for me?'

'It's hard to believe you'd get up in the early hours to do so. And how did you get into the café anyway?' Mel's attention was back on him. 'Break in?'

'Back door. It's easy to jimmy open. Jody and I used to break into the place when it was a sweet shop back in the day and nick a few lollies.'

'You didn't!' Mel's eyes went huge with shock. 'I can't believe I'm engaged to a juvenile delinquent.'

Tony shrugged. 'We did. Until we got caught. Luckily the local cop at the time put it down to us being traumatised by mum's death so let us off with a warning.'

'So, were you? Traumatised?'

Tony laced his fingers together and pushed them outwards in a stretch, hoping the action would keep him calm. He'd been young when his mother had died, but he hadn't been dumb. He'd missed her fiercely, stolen hankies from her drawer and slept with them at night. Not that he'd ever admitted that to anyone, not that he ever would. His business always ended up town business, but the love he'd had for his mum, the misery he'd felt at her passing, that was his and his only. And part of him was terrified that if he shared that misery he'd lose his last connection with her. He released the stretch. 'I was hardly old enough to be traumatised. Confused perhaps. Maybe Jodes was traumatised, but I just knew that Mummy had gone away and wasn't coming back.'

'Explains a lot.' Mel propped her elbows up on the table and cradled her chin in her hands.

'Really? Does it now?' Tony leant forward in his chair to see what drop of 'I get you, Tony' wisdom was about to come from Mel's lips.

'You can't commit to a woman because you're afraid you'll be left alone again, so you commit to the pub because it can't leave. It doesn't take a psych student to figure that one out.' Mel sat back in her chair and crossed her arms, a satisfied half-smile on her lips.

She had a point, but he knew that already. She'd only scratched the surface, though.

'Aren't you going to get grumpy with me for sussing you out?' The half-smile had disappeared, replaced with little vertical lines of irritation running between her brows.

'What's to grump about? I'm quite sure having your mother die on you at such an age would have a profound impact on any young person. But if you want to figure me out, you're going to have to go deeper than that.'

Mel unfolded her arms, then folded them again. Her forehead screwed up in thought. 'For a simple man, Tony McArthur, you're really quite difficult.'

Tony necked his latte and put the cup down. 'Good. Now get up. Break time's over and your mum looks ready to come over here and grab us by our ears.'

'I heard that,' Valerie called out. 'And you're right.'

'Are we still on for my next cooking lesson?' Tony stood up and rolled his shoulders in an attempt to loosen his cricked-up muscles. Being hunkered over a sink for hours and hours was crampy work. 'I got the lamb shanks this time. Thank God your mum sold so many steak dinners last night, because the butcher looked ready to toss me out if I didn't have the cash.'

'The butcher's a wise man. And you'd better believe we're on for another cooking lesson. It's not just lamb shanks either… I'm also teaching you how to make freshly crumbed fish today. I refuse to see anyone eat that frozen "fish" ever again. The pub's too good. She deserves better than that.'

Tony smiled. Mel had acknowledged the pub properly. '*She*'. So she had been listening last night. And she understood.

Good.

***

'Thanks for today, Mum.' Mel collected the empty food trays into a tidy pile for washing.

'Well, it wasn't like I had a choice, but you know I actually rather enjoyed myself.' Valerie squeezed Mel's shoulder as she waltzed past with the mop, cleaning the floors while humming a vaguely balletic tune.

'I didn't know you could bake?'

'I am your grandmother's daughter, am I not? You weren't the only one she taught her tricks to.'

Mel nodded. Of course her grandmother had taught her mother. Baking was the one thing her gran had been passionate about. Her cakes and biscuits had even won prizes at their local agricultural and pastoral show, much to all the 'proper' ladies' chagrin. The idea that a single mother who had no desire to marry ever again could beat them in a baking contest had led to much behind-the-hand gossiping, much to her gran's delight.

'Let them talk about me,' she'd cackled to Mel as she'd creamed eggs and sugar for yet another cake. 'Shows how sad their lives are. Now, Mel, what's the name of your mother's latest boyfriend?'

Yes, baking had been her gran's passion. And Mel's saviour.

'So I've been chatting with a couple of the locals at the pub and it seems that this engagement of yours hasn't been properly celebrated.' Valerie stopped cleaning the floors and leant on the mop, one elegant eyebrow raised in question.

Ice water ran through Mel's veins. The game was up. Her mother was going to demand answers, find out the truth and then force her out in search of a man. Two men. One for each of them.

'Well, to be honest, until you put that notice in the paper we'd kept everything pretty quiet. Wanted to avoid being gossiped about...'

'Oh, don't I just. But what's there to gossip about? Two

young and attractive people falling in love and wanting to spend their lives together is a wonderful thing. So I've decided to host your engagement party. We'll hold it at Tony's after the rugby match. That way, win or lose, there's something to celebrate.'

Mel gripped the counter, her knuckles white with tension.

'You don't have to do that. Honestly, Mum. We're happy being low-key about the whole thing. Heck, we'd planned to just do a registry wedding. Nothing big. Nothing out there.'

'Says the girl with bright-pink hair.'

'Besides, it's only two days away…'

'I know. But the venue is sorted. I've asked the visiting rugby players to blow up balloons in exchange for a batch of brownies and the Rotary ladies have agreed to whip up sandwiches and savouries. They were very happy to finally hear of your engagement, you know. I had no idea Tony was such a man about town. It seems they no longer feel they have to keep their daughters locked up. I'm sure they were just joking, though…'

More like telling the absolute truth. Mel closed her eyes and drew in a long, slow breath. This was a fait accompli. Hurricane Val had decided to do something and there was no way she could stop her. But that didn't mean she couldn't try.

'Well that's very kind of you, Mum, but aren't you

meant to be on holiday? I'm sure it's not too late to cancel the plans and, you know, put your feet up for the rest of your stay.'

Her mother shook her head and clucked her tongue. 'Oh, you know me, Mel. I get bored. And besides, it'll give me a chance to wear a nice dress and show off my dance moves in front of the captain of the Babbler team. I'm pretty sure he's interested. And there's no ring on his finger. I checked. Anyway…' Valerie flapped the conversation away with a wave of her hand. 'Enough about that, the engagement party is on. But we clearly need to talk about that wedding of yours. I'm sure you don't really plan on having a registry office wedding. No, you'll be doing it right. We'll need to look at dresses and shoes, decide on cakes, the guest list, food… I know you'd try to, but there's no way I'll allow you to self-cater. And don't tell me the reception's going to be at the pub? That would hardly be romantic. Fine enough for an engagement party, but nowhere near beautiful enough for the wedding of the year.'

Wedding of the year? Mel's mouth dried out. She tried to lick her lips, but nada. It was a drought in there.

'We… well, we…' She swallowed. How was she going to stop her mother from organising an engagement party *and* a wedding? 'We're probably not going to get married for a couple of years. Tony's busy. Money's tight. We're just taking it easy. It's not like we're in a hurry. After all, we've got the rest of our lives to get married...' She laughed. Weak. Unconvincing.

Her mother's eyes squinted. She smelt a rat.

'A lot can happen in a couple of years, Melanie.'

Uh-oh. She was 'Melanie' again. That meant her mother was about to dig her heels in and get her own way.

'If I were you I'd be getting that ring on his finger and settling down good and proper. I'd stop with the sleeping-here-some-nights arrangement, too. Who knows where that could lead to? Or what. Or who...'

A spark of anger flickered deep in Mel's gut. Who did her mother think she was? Coming in here and taking over? Telling Mel how to live her life? It wasn't as if she had set a good example by living a good life herself. Flitting from town to town, man to man. Ignoring Mel's protests whenever she brought a new man to Gran's to once again tell them she was in love, getting married, and that Mel was to be moving out of Gran's and in with them immediately. It was time her mother learned that her way was not the only way.

'Sure, Mum. I'll hurry up and get that ring on his finger. It's clearly the best thing to do. I mean it worked out so well for you. How many times?'

Tension churned in the air. Her mother's demeanour changed from determined to down-right diamond-tough.

'You don't talk to me like that. I am your mother.'

'And I am a grown woman capable of making her own decisions.'

'Capable? Really?'

'I have my own business.' Mel tilted her chin in defiance. Daring her mother to deny that truth.

'A tiny café in a tinier town? You don't even own the building. You could be turfed out at any second.'

Mel could've laughed. Her mother had no idea. In a quiet village like Rabbits Leap the landlords were grateful for a regular rent check. It wasn't like there were people begging to move here and start up businesses....

'As for marrying a man with a rundown shack for a pub? Is that really how you want to spend your life? Working here so you can prop up his vanity project?'

Fury flooded through her. It was one thing for a woman who'd spent her life making mistake after mistake to judge her lifestyle, but to bring Tony into it? Tony was doing everything he could to keep his bar relevant, including pretending to be engaged to her and putting up with her harridan mother.

'You do not say a word against Tony if you want to stay living in my apartment one more second. He works harder every single day than most people do in a week. That pub isn't just his job, it's his life, his home.'

'And you think that's the right man to marry? A man who'll spend his days and nights serving other people instead of spending time with you?'

'What do you think he did today, Mother? He could have stayed at The Bullion all morning if he'd wanted to. Could've slept the day away in preparation for another big night looking after the men who bring him one decent cash injection every two years. But he didn't. He saw I needed sleep and he took it upon himself to let me have it.' Mel clenched her fists at her side, digging her nails into her palm, hoping the pain would release the anger that was threatening to overwhelm her. 'Tony cares about me. More than you ever have.'

'I care.' Valerie's chin tilted in defiance.

'You didn't care enough. You dumped me on Gran's doorstep more times than I can count on one hand. And it wasn't for my own good. It was for yours. Every. Single. Time. I've known Tony for a far shorter time and he's already shown me what caring looks like. He's a loyal man, a good man. He's worth more than all of your men put together.'

A shadow crossed Valerie's face. She looked down at her feet. Her shoulders hitched up, down. Up again. And down. She looked up, her face unreadable. 'I'll confirm the catering for the engagement party. Then we'll start sorting out your wedding. Well, I'm going to take a shower. I never got to have one this morning... I was too busy helping you.'

Mel watched her mother trudge up the stairs and wished for the millionth time that she could disengage herself from this whole mess. Whether she liked it or not, her mother was invested in her new-found happiness. At this rate she was going to have to marry Tony. Or find a believable way to get out of it.

But how?

CHAPTER SEVEN

'Is there enough wine in this bar to make today disappear?'

Tony looked up from whisking batter for that evening's fish and chips special to see a very drawn Mel standing in front of him. Bruise-coloured rings under her eyes. Skin pale as a mid-winter frost. Hair scraped back off her face with a headband. Shoulders slumped over in what looked like defeat. 'What do you mean? What's happened?'

Mel arched an eyebrow.

He nodded in understanding. It wasn't a case of what, so much as 'who'. 'Geez, I leave you two girls alone for five minutes and all hell breaks loose.'

'More like a conversation happens.'

'Big one from the looks of it.'

Mel nodded and lowered her head onto the bar so her cheek was resting on it, her eyes looking up at him, so tired, so haunted. 'You have no idea.'

'So, what happened between you two?'

She clapped her hand over her visible eye and sighed.

'Well, let's put it this way… not only do you now have a fiancé, and a future mother-in-law, but there's also to be an engagement party this Saturday…'

Engagement party? What the hell?

'The Rotary ladies are catering and she's already got it sorted. I think it's part of some plan for her to snap up the captain of the opposing team or something. It's not really about us. Or me. It never is.'

Mel's hand slipped away. She looked beaten and Tony suspected the mother-daughter conversation had been a little more serious than just engagement talk.

'Screw the drink, I have a better idea.' Vaulting over the bar he picked Mel up and cradled her against his chest.

'Put me down, you caveman.' She struggled to escape his grip, a frown wrinkling her brow. 'I don't know what you're planning to do with me, but I want nothing to do with it.'

'You'll do as you're told, woman. This once, anyway.' He muttered and tightened his grip.

He marched her through the bar door, past the kitchen and up the stairs to his room, with her mewling and wriggling the whole way. It was like herding sheep. But harder. Mel sure had spirit.

He liked that.

He kicked open the bedroom door and surveyed the room. Rumpled bed. Curtains still drawn. Yesterday's clothing still unwashed. Usually by now the bed would be made, curtains pulled, window open for fresh air. You could tell he was distracted.

Speaking of distraction. He had a job to do.

'I'm serious, Tony. This is not cool. You can't make me do anything I don't want to do.'

There was fear in those words. Fear in her eyes, too. Did she think he was going to…?

He walked over and carefully laid Mel onto the bed.

'Tony. No.' Tears had built up. Were threatening to spill.

He took her shoes off, one by one, and pulled the blankets up over her.

'There you go. Now get some sleep. This morning's sleep-in obviously wasn't enough. You look like you could do with four thousand winks.'

Mel inhaled, then exhaled, as if she were fighting some internal battle, trying to regain control of herself. She swiped at her eyes.

'I thought you were going to…'

'What?' Tony smoothed the blankets beside her and sat on the bed. 'Bring you up here and force you to do something untoward with me?'

A small nod.

What had happened to Mel to make her believe a man would act like that? The obvious answer came to mind but Tony knocked it away. Surely not? But maybe it would explain her careful, sensible attitude to life, her need to be in control of everything around her…

He took Mel's headband off and set it on the bedside table. 'I would never do that. Not to you. Not to any woman. It would be abhorrent. It's just I can see things are getting on top of you. You're at work in the café all day. You're helping me in the kitchen at night. And you're dealing with that mother of yours, which I suspect isn't easy. When do you ever rest? When do you ever sleep?'

Mel yawned, her eyes getting heavier.

'You helped me this morning,' she murmured, the words heavy with exhaustion.

'It was the least I could do. Now get some sleep.' He dropped a kiss on her forehead and walked backwards out of the room so he could watch sleep take over. See Mel transform from an overworked young woman into a dozing angel.

Dozing angel? When did he get so romantic? Maybe he needed to get some kip himself. He eyed the other side of the bed, then shook his head. No time to kip. He had a dinner service to prepare. A hungry team of rugby players to feed. And apparently, an engagement party to sort out.

***

The sun slipped through a wrinkled crack of the curtains, striking Mel in the eyes.

'It's too early,' she mumbled into the pillow. And she didn't want to get up. She was having a nice dream. Playing with lambs in fields. Daffodils bobbing around her. Tony holding his own lamb and feeding it from a bottle, looking up at her, giving her a smile and wink. Her knees went as wobbly as a newborn lamb as she sank next to him and…

Lambs. Lamb burgers. Patties. She was meant to have shown Tony how to make them, and she'd slept through the night. He'd never forgive her.

Mel bolted up out of bed and blinked, hard. Where was she again? Not at home. Tony's. She was in his room. But why? And shouldn't the sun have been in the east? His bedroom faced west. What was going on?

The gentle clink of glasses and murmur of voices wafted up through the wooden floorboards. So it wasn't morning after all, which meant she'd have time to help Tony with the dinner service.

Grabbing her shoes she flew down the stairs into the kitchen. Rich, warm, meaty aromas filled the usually cold kitchen air.

'Feel better?'

Tony stood at the oven, three frying pans crowding the hotplate, each filled with burger patties, already golden brown on one side. Another pot bubbled away merrily as something boiled inside.

She glanced over at the kitchen bench to see a perfectly

chopped coleslaw glistening with a herbaceous-smelling dressing. Then noticed the oven door was glowing orange. What did he have in there?

Rushing to the door in curiosity, she nudged him over, opened the door and looked in. It was the lamb shanks, in a rich-looking gravy. She pulled open the cutlery drawer, blindly fished for a spoon, then dipped it into the gravy, brought it to her mouth, blew on it to cool it down and then tasted. Tomatoes, red wine, beef stock, rosemary, well seasoned.

'Has my mother been here?'

Tony threw his head back and laughed, revealing perfectly straight white teeth. *All the better to nibble on her with?* Mel swatted the idea away. That daft dream had obviously left her more open to Tony's charms than usual. Who knew teeth could be attractive?

'She's out front serving customers.'

'So she did help?'

'What if I said she did?' He took her hand and pulled her up.

'Then that would explain a lot.' His hand was still on hers. She really ought to pull it away, especially now that he'd tugged her a little bit closer to him.

'What if I said she didn't?'

Mel gulped as he drew her nearer still. Was that searing heat coming from him or the oven? Or from some place deep within herself?

'If you said she didn't I'd be tempted to think you weren't telling the truth…'

'Call me a liar, because she didn't. And that is the truth. I did it all myself. Proud of me?'

His eyes twinkled as he dipped his head closer to hers, his lips quirked in a smile. Could you kiss through a smile, Mel half wondered as his lips pressed upon hers. Warm, yet tough, with the potential to be very demanding. His arm slipped around her waist and brought her closer, erasing the space between them. Ravenous, she deepened the kiss, his mouth giving way so she could explore. Their tongues slipping around each other. Salty, tangy, with that earthy scent of hops. She could taste him all day. All night.

His hand skirted her lower back, dipped lower…

A low moan filled the kitchen. Someone was hungry? They could wait. She was busy. Hold on. That was her.

The realisation threw icy-cold water on her wants, her needs. She broke away and tried to ignore Tony's look of bewilderment.

She shouldn't be doing this. Not with Tony. And it wasn't even that he was only good for a fling and that she wasn't into that kind of man. It wouldn't be fair on him. She was the kind of girl who would want more. A settled, simple life. He wouldn't be able to give it to her and things would just get messy between them. No, the less complications this arrangement had, the better. As far as Mel was concerned, the only things allowed to get hot in this kitchen were the plates of food, and that was it.

'I'm sorry. I shouldn't have...' Tony left the words hanging as if he didn't know what he should be sorry for.

'No. It's not you. Really.' And it wasn't. It was all her. Her need for security. Her desire for love. She picked up the spatula and flipped the burgers, then turned off the hotplates so they wouldn't burn. Grabbing a wooden spoon she opened the oven door and stirred the gravy, not caring that it slopped over the sides and sizzled on the bottom of the oven.

'Mel...' He tentatively touched her shoulder. She shrugged it off, ignoring the comforting warmth it brought.

'What?' She stood up and tossed the spoon into the sink.

'I don't understand what's going on here.' His eyes searched hers, looking for answers.

What could she tell him? That she was about to ruin his life? That he was going to be stuck with her for possibly the better part of forever if her mother was determined to stick around not only for an engagement party but then the wedding, so as to ensure Mel sealed the deal? Or worse, he'd have to ruin his reputation for being a good guy, a gentleman, by being the one to break off the engagement? Sure, she could do it, but it wouldn't be realistic. He was the flighty one, the playboy. The town wouldn't like it, but they'd maybe understand it. And then what? They'd go back to being casual acquaintances... or worse, awkward strangers who crossed the street when they saw the other one coming? A dull pang thudded through her heart. Could she go back to a life without Tony in it? That wasn't a life she wanted. The realisation hit her like a twenty-five-pound bag of flour.

So that was the problem? This was why she kept swinging between wanting him and wanting to be nowhere near him? She had feelings for Tony? Feelings beyond general attraction that any woman with a pair of eyes would feel when they looked at the Tony-shaped package? Her mind raced. When had this happened? How? Bile rose up in Mel's throat. This hadn't been part of the plan.

'Order in!' The pub door swung open, her mother's voice filled the tense air. 'Four lamb burgers, two fish, two shanks. And don't dilly-dally about it, you two love birds. The boys are hungry tonight!'

Mel let out a sigh of relief. They had work to do. Work meant keeping busy, not thinking, and most importantly, having a distraction to help her resist every fibre in her being that wanted to pin Tony against the kitchen wall, any wall, and kiss him again.

'You sort out the burgers and fish. I'll mash the potatoes and serve up the lamb,' she ordered, swinging into action.

'Yes, Ma'am.' He saluted her with a grin. Only a half-one, though. That guilt-inducing confusion still surrounded him, even as he got to work. Broad shoulders hunched, a crease upon his brow, his jaw working every now and then as if he wanted to say something, but didn't know where to begin.

'So you really did all this yourself? No help from my mum?' Maybe getting back to the original topic of conversation would normalise this strange situation.

'Yep.'

Okay. He'd gone monosyllabic on her. She could work with that.

'How'd you manage that? The gravy is really good. Like sop-it-up-with-bread good.'

He nodded to the counter, where an old recipe book lay. Mel picked it up and opened its age-worn cover. Carefully she turned each page, taking in recipe after recipe, each carefully written out in beautiful cursive, the odd strike-through where the author had figured out a way to improve on the recipes. And oh, what food they'd cooked. Hearty, rich, using affordable meats and slow-cooking them until they would have melted from the bone. Humble yet rich, self-saucing desserts. This wasn't a recipe book, it was a treasure trove.

'Where did you find this? It's amazing.'

'It was my mum's.'

Tony set the plates under the heat lamps and started mashing the potatoes that Mel had completely forgotten about.

'I'm sorry, that was my job…'

'It's okay.' He turned his back to her, leaving her to continue reading the book.

'She was very talented.' She looked up to see him shrug. 'Why haven't you used these before?'

Tony placed the bowls of shanks next to the burgers, hit the bell for service, then turned to Mel. His face was unreadable. Blank. The sparkle in his eyes had died.

'It didn't feel like mine. It felt like it was waiting for the right person to come along.'

The right person? Did he mean her? That's why it had been dusted off? Yet he'd been the one to do the cooking. And cook he could. The divine lamb shank stew was proof of that.

'Well, it looks like you were the right person, if that meal you made was anything to go by.' She held up her hand for a buddy-buddy high five. And waited. Waited some more. No slap of 'yeah, I'm awesome' was forthcoming. Instead, Tony leant back on the counter, crossed his arms and raised two very unimpressed eyebrows. Was now the time to tell him about her mother's plans? It wasn't like things could get much more awkward between them…

'Tony, we have to talk.'

'Aren't we already?'

Mel swallowed. 'Things have got more… difficult… for you, me. I mean, us.'

'More difficult? How could anything get more difficult? It already feels like we're between a rock and a hard place.'

'Well, there's no easy way to say this, so I'm just going to say it... Mum's not going anywhere. She's staying here a little longer than a few weeks. She may be here a few months. That chat I had with her today, she wants to do more than organise an engagement party... She wants to stick around to sort out the wedding, too. Make sure I get that ring on your finger...' She held her breath and waited for the fury. For the reprimands. The pointed finger of doom.

Tony unfolded his arms. Folded them again. Crossed one leg over the other.

'Okay.'

Two letters. Two syllables. Both sounded calm. Controlled. Was Tony... *okay* with this whole charade? Did he still want to carry it on?

'We can find a way to get out of this.' Mel gulped. Maybe he hadn't heard right? 'I thought maybe you could break up with me since, you know, you don't do commitment. Or if that doesn't suit we could just suck it up and admit the truth? I mean, you don't even need me any more. That recipe book in your hands is a goldmine. You'll have millionaires flying their little planes into local fields to get a taste of that goodness.'

Mel paused and waited for Tony to nod his head in agreement. He didn't.

'Or we could say we've drifted apart? That the pressure of running two businesses got to us?' She fished about for excuses they could use. Why wasn't he agreeing? She was giving him an out. He should be jumping on it.

Did he just smirk? Was he enjoying this?

'I don't know, Mel.' Tony uncrossed his arms and lifted them up in a languorous stretch, revealing a hint of that toned stomach she'd glimpsed the night before. 'If we break up, what will happen to you? Will your mother drag you all over the place looking for a man? I mean, that's why all this happened, isn't it? To avoid having to be a wing-man to the world's most eager cougar? Or maybe it's more that she'll also be trying to find you a man as well? And we couldn't have that, could we, Mel? Allowing yourself to meet a good guy, a guy who'd stick around and treat you well. It's better, safer, to date those who will probably leave anyway.'

What was he saying? And why? Did he really believe she was incapable of loving a man? That she only got into relationships that were doomed to fail?

'The men I date do treat me well.'

'But they don't stick around.'

'And would you? Would you stick around?' If he was going to push her buttons, she'd push back. Harder.

'I don't know? Would I? Would you let me? Or would you push me away like you're doing right now? You can't keep pushing everyone away forever, Mel. You'll end up old and alone and wishing you could have made a different choice in a pub kitchen forty years ago.'

Mel glanced down at her feet, unable to handle his knowing gaze one microsecond longer. What was happening here? Was Tony trying to tell her he wanted to be with her? That he was willing to give up his love 'em and leave 'em ways for her? Or was he just trolling her? Was that his way of getting back at her for forcing him into a tight corner? A corner she'd just given him a chance to get out of?

'I'll say it once more. We can end this thing now. I'll take the blame. It can be on my head.'

She glanced up. He'd gone. The gentle swinging of the door the only proof he'd been here at all.

Yeah, he'd leave. That's why there was no point falling for Tony McArthur.

CHAPTER EIGHT

'Well, that's that done for the night.' Mel untied the pinafore, lifted it over her head and draped it over a barstool. 'I do believe I require a drink. Pinot... of the noir variety, please.'

Tony nodded, grabbed the bottle and twisted the cap, watching the ruby-red liquid fill up to the age-worn line that told the rookies to stop pouring. He added in an extra glug. Two. She deserved it. Mel had worked so hard, pushing out orders, delivering orders, picking up plates and getting them washed, all without a word of a complaint.

'Here.' Mel held out her bank card.

'Oh no.' Tony waved the offending card away. 'This is on the house. The next one, too.'

'What? You're not going to charge me? Are you sure? I mean there's that hole in your truck's muffler that needs fixing. And don't get me started on that bed of yours...'

'After you worked all night? I'm a hard taskmaster, but I'm not completely evil. Besides, those meals you've showed me how to make are actually making me money. I paid off the butcher in full today. The power company's next. Soon I'll be able to afford to put the heating on again.'

A warm glow filled Tony as Mel rewarded him with a smile. And not one of the cursory, tight, small ones she'd been giving him since their conversation in the kitchen earlier. Or the grimace he'd seen when he'd carried her to bed earlier that day, when she'd seemed scared, so unlike the brave little trooper he had come to know. What had caused that fear? That overreaction to a simple act of kindness? Something wasn't right. Tony debated bringing it up, but he didn't want to lose that smile. A smile that reached Mel's eyes, warming the brown hues to an almost amber colour. From a dark stout to a light lager. An idea tingled in the back of his mind.

'What do you reckon about this whole craft beer fad?' He screwed the cap back on the wine bottle and set it aside.

'Fad? Haven't people been brewing their own beer for ever?'

'Yeah, but it's gone a level above that. It's a bit like what's happened to coffee... Coffee's not two spoonfuls of instant and a bit of hot water any more and beer's no longer men drinking the equivalent of petrol in their homes to save a few bucks. I've been reading a lot lately about all these fellows in the cities getting into boutique beers – you know, pale ales, pilsners, porters…'

'I think it's a great idea if it's done right.' Mel's finger circled the wine glass. 'Why? Are you thinking of getting into it?'

'Maybe. I mean, I brew a bit, here and there. Just a small hobby…'

'Really? You kept that quiet.'

'Well, I only bring my efforts out on the odd occasion, you know, when I feel like treating the regulars, and they've always been quite complimentary about it. I'm just wondering if maybe there's a business idea there.'

Mel sat up straighter in her seat. 'Do you have some here? Can I try it?'

'I've never known you to drink beer?'

'Well, I've never known myself to get engaged, work eighteen-hour days, some of them for free, and teach all my culinary secrets to a man I barely know, so maybe I'm in the mood to try new things.'

Mel was in the mood to try new things? Did he count? Was she finally ready to have a little fun? Or was she only talking about the beer? Tony gently bounced up and down on his feet, pondering his options.

Mel's eyebrows rose in expectation and impatience. 'Are you going to get the beer or are you going to wait for me to be on the edge of death from thirst so I'm guaranteed to like it?'

Beer. She was just talking about the beer. Bugger. 'Yeah, yeah, calm your farm, I'll go get it. Be back in a tick.'

Tony sprinted up the stairs to his small lounge. He opened the door of the little bar fridge he kept next to the sofa, pulled out two bottles of his latest brews, his best yet, and raced down the stairs, two at a time.

'That was quick. Did you think I'd leave?' Mel pushed the wine glass away.

'Nah,' Tony puffed. He set the bottles carefully on the bar, grabbed an opener and lifted the cap off the first. 'I just didn't want you falling asleep on the bar before you could try these. I also didn't want to lug you up the stairs twice in one day. My poor back couldn't handle it.' He laughed at Mel's withering glance.

'So what have you got for me, my six-feet-tall, muscle-bound weakling?' Mel picked up one of the bottles and inspected the label he'd created on his computer and printed off. It featured a Hereford cow munching freesias – a nod to his grandparents' favourite breed of cow and his mother's favourite flowers.

Taking the bottle from her, he opened it and poured the beer into a glass, held on an angle to ensure there wasn't too much of a head. 'This would be a pale ale of the American variety. A little malty, some caramel notes, a touch of fruitiness…'

Mel brought the glass up to her nose and sniffed. 'You sound like a sommelier.'

'Well, a good beer is every bit as interesting as a good wine. It's not all just brown stuff to wash the day away, you know.'

Mel sipped. Tony watched her face, waiting for a reaction. There was none. She took another sip. Still no reaction. His pulse picked up. Did she hate it? Another sip. A gulp. Okay. She didn't hate it. If it were putrid she'd have spat it out by now or pushed the glass back in his direction.

'This is insane.' Mel took another sip.

'Insane? As in good insane? Insanely good insane?'

Mel pushed the empty glass in his direction. 'Why are you serving this swill...' She indicated the line-up of beers on tap. 'When you could be selling this?'

'You know, Mel. That's what I've been thinking. Now, try this.' He poured a glass of dark, chocolatey stout, his favourite winter brew, into a fresh glass.

Mel sipped. 'Mmmmmm. Oh my.' Her eyes closed in enjoyment as she took another sip. 'It's like... sex in a beer. I want to swim in it. Lap it up. Feel it roll over my body. I bet it would be like sleeping in a bed of silk.'

Tony's pulse picked up again. So did something else. He'd never seen Mel so... ecstatic. So excited. So sexy.

He poured himself a half of the stout and took a sip. Tasted like the same old stout as usual. No one had spiked it with one of those pills designed to cause arousal. Not that he needed one right now. Seeing Mel enjoying...

enjoying? Seeing Mel *revelling* in his own creation was all the aphrodisiac he needed.

'Do they all taste this good?' Her finger ran up the length of the glass, trailing through the condensation.

Tony gulped as his mind went to other, more intimate, places. 'I'd like to think so. So you like them?'

'Tony, you're an idiot.' Her eyes snapped open and fixed him with a frustrated glare. 'You are sitting on a goldmine and you don't even know it.'

'Well, I was thinking I could put a couple of my creations on tap… or in a bottle. Probably cheaper to chuck out than a whole keg's worth if it doesn't fly.'

'For one, there's no way this wouldn't fly. For two, I'm not just talking about the beer. Look at this place. It has space galore. This room, the one next door that's never used. It has a kitchen. You have been sitting on some of the finest recipes I've ever seen. And you can cook! You proved that this evening. Those lamb shanks – better than my own! The burgers. The fish. All excellent. You could turn this place around in a week or two if you put your mind to it. People would come from all over to eat your food and drink your brews.'

Tony could see where she was going, but he didn't want to head there. Change The Bullion? Fancy it up? Transform it from a spot for locals to somewhere outsiders could come and enjoy? Yeah, it made sense. He wasn't daft. But…

'Do you really think this is what your father would have wanted?'

Mel had read his mind.

'To see this building crumble? To see it stand still in time? An ode to yesteryear?'

An ode to yesteryear? No, it was more than that. The Bullion had become a memorial to the person his father had loved more than anyone in the world, and Tony felt it was his job to respect his father's last wishes and keep The Bullion's essence. To show his father, even in death, how much he'd respected him.

His father had worked day and night to provide for his family, to make sure they were secure. He may not have shown them much affection or ever said he loved them, but Tony knew that wasn't because he didn't have love or affection for them; it just wasn't his father's style. A roughing up of their hair, a wink here and there. That was his style. Besides, The Bullion had become a living embodiment of his father's love for his wife. *Keep her the same*, he'd told Tony in breathy gasps as he lay on the pub floor the night his heart had given out. *She's all we have left of her.* Her. His mother. He'd nodded in understanding, promised he would. And he'd kept that promise. He'd *keep* that promise, until his own last breath.

'I know what you're saying. I know where you're coming from. But to change this old girl that drastically?' He thought back to those final words. The promise

151

he'd made to keep The Bullion going. He'd made that promise not knowing the state of the finances. He'd seen the drop-off in customers. Asked about it. But his father had brushed him off, told him things were fine.

But they were anything but. Tony knew he had to change things, but what if those changes broke that last promise? What if those changes caused The Bullion to morph into something unrecognisable? What if he lost his few precious memories of his mother in the process?

Tony poured himself a glass of the stout, took a sip and rolled the full-bodied flavour around his mouth as he gazed over his domain. Maybe he could revamp the place without making it into something his father wouldn't have recognised. There was potential here. But there was money to consider and his budget was non-existent. Although... he could sand back and revarnish the tops of the leaners and the bar himself. The local seamstress could probably do him a deal on recovering the bar stools in a nicer fabric. Maybe even whip up some new curtains.

'I'm taking it by the way you're beginning to smile that I've got through to you?' Mel propped her chin up on her hand and smiled wearily.

Had she got through to him? Yeah. Hell, yeah. In more ways than he'd ever expected. He could see a whole new future ahead of him. A brighter future. The Bullion would be restored to her former glory. He could start a side business with his beer brewing. Maybe even finally knock up a beer garden out back. Make the place more appealing during the warmer months. And Mel? Well, maybe she'd hang around a little longer. If she'd have him.

'Mel...' He set his glass down and picked up her hand. So small. So warm. So much righter than he ever thought anything could feel. 'The day you forced me into a fake engagement....'

'You mean the day you decided to try and destroy my business by planning on selling coffee...' The words were teasing, her cheekbones lifted high in a suppressed smile.

'Well, I suppose you could look at it that way. But with hindsight I was getting the pointier end of the stick...'

'Yeah, yeah. We'll see about that when you're the most successful pub owner this district has ever seen...'

'You think I can do it?' He searched her eyes, looking for any hint of doubt.

'Of course. I know you can. If you can create food that makes my eyes water with jealousy, I know you can do anything.' She squeezed his hand.

A flood of happiness rolled through him, lifting the weight he'd felt for so long off his chest. So this was what the support of a good woman felt like. Was this how his father felt when he told his mother he wasn't going to farm like the rest of his family, that he was going to be a publican? A risky venture that could've seen them destitute. Or at the very least living in the little cottage with his parents for the rest of their lives. Did his mother make his father feel like he could take on the world? Because that was what Mel was making him feel right about now as she stared at him, eyebrows lifted in impatience. Waiting for him to do something... anything. But what? Oh.

'As I was saying before I was so rudely interrupted...' Tony walked around the bar to where Mel was seated and positioned himself in front of her. She spun round on the bar stool to fully face him, legs ever so slightly spread, elbows leant back, propping her up on the bar. She was the picture of contentment. Gone was the angst she'd had earlier in the kitchen. Maybe she was too tired to be uptight. Or maybe she'd decided he wasn't worth fighting. Or that he was worth being around... in a very un-business-arrangement manner. 'The day you forced me into that fake engagement...' He laid his hands on each of her thighs and brought his head level with hers. 'Was the best damn day I've had in nearly a decade.'

Blue eyes held Mel transfixed. Sparkling like the sea, but calm, unruffled. How could Tony look at her like this? Like a man who adored her. So unlike the looks she'd experienced from her mother's men. From the one who'd tried to hurt her. Yet, there was a similarity. A desire. A hunger. She turned her head from Tony so he couldn't kiss her.

'Mel?'

His breath was hot on her cheek. His confusion clear. 'What's wrong?'

'Nothing's wrong.' She stared at the coffee machine, sitting on the far end of the bench. Stupid machine. If it hadn't been for its existence she'd never have got herself into this mess. She'd never have found herself experiencing this uncomfortable level of warmth towards the man standing in front of her, his eyes fastened upon her. She could almost feel them willing her to look back at him.

'Is this to do with earlier? What happened up in the bedroom? You seemed kind of terrified up there.'

Had she been that obvious? Had the fear she'd tried to keep contained for so long not just trickled through but overflowed? Her heart rate picked up as she recalled how he'd grabbed her, how her survival instinct had kicked in when memories of unwanted touches and looks had been thrust upon her, the need to be in control of the situation, of her body, her life.

Mel bit her lip. Tony deserved to know why she was acting so odd. Why one minute she was hot for him, the second minute running off scared. Closing her eyes, she took a deep breath and exhaled.

'Things weren't easy for me growing up.'

There was a scraping of metal against floorboard as Tony pulled a chair up. A rush of cool air as he gave her space.

'Mum and I moved a lot. A new town, a new city for

every new man she found herself. Some of them were okay, I suppose. Others...' She shuddered as images of bloodshot eyes and chunky fingers sprang to mind. 'Others had a similar interest in me that they did my mother. One in particular.'

Mel forced herself to open her eyes, to face Tony. She expected to see her self-loathing reflected in his expression. But it wasn't there. Only compassion. Tenderness. She took another breath in and willed herself to go on.

'I'd told Mum he'd been looking at me wrong, that he was always walking in on me half-undressed, but she wouldn't listen. Said I was imagining things. One time she even accused me of trying to ruin her happiness.' Mel shook her head in disgust. 'Then one day, when she was away at work, he finally got drunk enough to do something. Staggered into my room, breathing his cheap beer stench.'

'Mel...' Tony's voice was low, urgent. 'You don't have to go on. You can stop.'

'I have to, don't you understand? If I don't face this, how can I ever be more than what I am? How could anyone lo... accept me?'

Tony nodded in acknowledgement and sat forward in the stool, his forearm on his knee, his hand outreached, open. Like an invitation for her to take it should she need an anchor.

'He tried to get at me, but I kicked him off. He tried

again. Chased me around my room until I was cornered. He began to rip at my pyjamas and then I heard the front door squeak open. To this day I don't know what caused Mum to come home earlier than usual from work, but she did and I screamed. And screamed. She came running, found him backing off, blaming me. Saying I came on to him.' Even after all this time the memory was still bitter in Mel's mind, the words sour in her mouth. 'Mum wasn't completely stupid, though. She finally saw through him and hauled us both out of there. Left the town, dumped me at Gran's and ran off to find another life. Not one I followed her to. I promised myself that would never happen again. That was when I was fifteen. At sixteen she came back to get me but I took off, left Gran's and ran away to Leeds. To safety. And then I found my way here.' *And now I've found you.*

'That bastard.'

Mel snapped her head up to see Tony's fists clenched at his side, his nostrils flaring.

'And your mother. How could she do that to you? How could she not believe you right from the start? And have you talked about any of this with her? Is that why you two look ready to go ten rounds in a ring half the time?'

Mel shrugged. 'All I ever wanted was for her to make me her number-one priority. Not some guy. You'd think it wouldn't be too much to ask, but apparently it is.' She reached for Tony's fists and held them in her hands. 'Don't be angry for me. Or sad for me. Just be here for me.' She angled her head upwards and brought her lips up to his.

'No, Mel.' Tony shook her hands off and held his up, putting distance between them. 'I can't. Not after what happened to you. Not after your'e told me that. It would be wrong. You need to talk to your mum. Clear the air. Start afresh.'

'No, now's not the time. Later. I promise.' Mel brought her hands up to Tony's and interlaced her fingers with his. 'As for now? Now, you and I, it would be right. I have never told anyone that story before. Never trusted anyone enough. But I trust you, Tony. With everything. With all of me.'

The fight went out of him, but a flame remained. His fingers closed over hers and he pulled her towards him.

'Are you sure?'

She curled her fingers around his neck, then brought his lips down to hers. He hesitated for a microsecond, then yielded. Soft, strong, delicious.

Mel brought him closer, deeper. Their tongues entwined, a perfect fit, tasting each other, wanting more, insatiable.

Tony trailed his fingers over the swell of her breasts, down her side. Mel moaned into his mouth and pushed hard up against him, wanting him more than she'd wanted anything in her life.

He broke contact. Indecision flashed across his handsome face, confirming what Mel had begun to understand. Tony McArthur was a good man, a true gentleman and, even if only for one night, she wanted him to be hers.

With a smile and a nod she gave him her answer.

***

Mel woke up to the dawn chorus of blackbirds and robins. They sounded just how she felt. Happy, full of light, ready to take on another day with a joyful heart. She glanced over at Tony, his bare arm curled around his pillow in a hug. The sheet tangled around his waist, giving her a good look at his broad chest, divinely defined abs, and the totally touchable curve of his lats.

Last night had been unexpected. The exact opposite of the self-imposed Tony ban. She should've been kicking herself right now for going to bed with a man she had feelings for, a man she knew could never feel the same way back because his love quota was taken up by the pub, his sister and his nephews, and anyone else was only there for a good and short time... but despite knowing that, she couldn't muster an iota of regret, because last night had been crazy wonderful.

She'd never known lovemaking to be so intimate. Tony had taken his time with her. Stroking, teasing, kissing every inch of her skin. Not going further until she'd all but begged and then he'd tipped her over to levels of ecstasy she'd never experienced, perhaps because for the first time in her life she'd been willing to allow someone to do so.

A seed of doubt planted itself in her happiness. It was madness to open herself up to someone with a reputation like his. To put herself at risk of being shafted when something newer came along.

And yet... she was no longer sure that the Tony she'd heard about was the Tony lying asleep in front of her. Something had shifted within him. There was a sincerity within that come-hitherness that hadn't been there before. After making love they'd talked about his plans, for a micro-brewery, for a menu that changed with the seasons. Menus she'd design. Mel's heart had bloomed with hope at the inclusion. Was there a chance of a good time and a long time?

No, Mel cautioned herself. It was better to take it day by day, to see where things went. Better not to open her heart completely in case he changed his mind, shut her out and left her scrambling to create a new life. Again.

***

'So, you two. We really should be setting a date for this wedding of yours.'

Mel rolled her eyes at Tony, glad her mother was too busy doing the last of the café's dishes to see her daughter's silent act of cheekiness.

'Shall we get over this engagement party first, Valerie?' Tony took a dry plate and stacked it on top of the tower in the cupboard.

'Well, Mel's not getting any younger and you'll be wanting to start a family. Buy a home. Settle down properly. A pub is no place to raise a family.'

Mel didn't have to be an expert on body language to know that her mother had just said the absolute wrong thing to Tony.

'I was raised in that pub and I think I came out okay.' His words were granite-hard, as were the muscles tensed beneath his T-shirt, his knuckles snow-white as they gripped another plate.

'Oh, I know you were fine. But it's just not what I'd want for my grandchildren. Who knows what they'd be exposed to in such a place?'

'Mum.' Mel kept her voice even while willing her mother to shut up.

'Drunk people and children are not a good mix,' her mother prattled on, oblivious to the flare of angst in the atmosphere.

Had Valerie really forgotten how often she'd put her own daughter in that very situation? Dragging her into bars far less wholesome than The Bullion, before she was of legal age? Laughing it off when the drunks made inappropriate comments about Mel's burgeoning curves. Surely she hadn't let it slip her mind. Tony was right. She and her mother needed to have a chat. To have it out once and for all. But when?

'And who knows what they'd grow up to think was normal?' Valerie wiped her wet hands on a tea towel and turned to Mel and Tony. 'Day drinking. Drunkenness. Debauchery...'

'Mother.' Mel kept her voice low, but firm. 'You need to stop talking.'

'Well, I'm only thinking about what's best for your children, Mel. Surely you want the best for them?'

'What I want is for you to keep out of our business. Tony and I will do what's right for us. And right now that involves going about our lives, working on our businesses, and doing whatever makes us happy.'

Tony's hand fell upon her shoulder. 'It's all right, Mel. Don't worry about it.'

'But I will and I do. Mum, I won't have you bulldozing us with your plans or airing your opinions all over the place without any regard for who you're speaking to. Tony grew up in The Bullion and he became a fine man. I have no doubt any child growing up there would, too.'

'Well, you don't have to be snippy about it, Melanie.'

Mel exhaled as her mother backed down and returned to doing the dishes.

'I just want to ensure your children have a better upbringing than you did.'

So that was what this was all about? A half-hearted

attempt by her mother to apologise for the past? A way to show she was sorry by ensuring her grandchildren weren't subjected to the same kind of life Mel had been? Mel nearly laughed out loud. That would never happen. Her children would have the opposite life to the one she'd grown up with. They'd know they were loved, know they were safe, know they were heard.

'Mel, do you have a minute?' Tony sounded serious. Had her mother's rudeness annoyed him so much he was going to call the whole thing off? Mel's stomach sickened at the thought. Her heart, too. She should've seen this coming... Shouldn't have told him the truth about her childhood. She should've known that once the haze of lust had blown over he'd be repulsed by her. More than anything, she shouldn't have allowed a tiny part of her to get its hopes up. She knew better than that.

'Sure.' She shrugged his hand off her shoulder and made for the doorway. 'Mum, we'll be upstairs.'

'Go ahead...' Valerie waved them away in a huff. 'Just leave me to do everything. As always.'

Mel fought the urge to roll her eyes again as she stalked up the stairs, Tony following close behind. She couldn't see him but that shadow her mother had cast still surrounded him.

'Come in.' She opened the door and waved him through. He stepped over the threshold, hands in jeans pockets, and looked around.

Her heart did a jitterbug. Could he be any more handsome? Any more manly? His presence filled the flat, making it seem even smaller. The vanilla-bean candle that emitted a sweet, sensual scent, even when unlit, was erased by his potent, hoppy, earthy aroma. She breathed it in. If he was going to call this whole thing quits she wanted to take that scent with her.

'This place feels like you.' Tony looked over at her, deep lines appearing around his eyes as the edges of his mouth lifted in a small smile.

Oh great, he was going to let her down gently. Be nice about it. Be the eternal gentleman everyone said he was. Making it impossible to hate him, even if he put a dent in her heart as he left.

'How so?' Mel swallowed and tried to ignore the traitorous heat surging low in her stomach. *Guard up, Mel.*

'It's warm. Welcoming. Quirky. Cute. It's the real you. Not the "you" you show the rest of the world.'

'Well, it's not like I'm hiding anything.'

'Not any more.'

'And I didn't hide anything last night.' Mel put on a brave smile. If he was going to show her the door there was no way she would show him her disappointment.

He laughed, a throaty chuckle that set the heat in the pit of her stomach on fire.

'No. You didn't.'

'So, what did you want to talk about?' Mel steadied her emotions and waited for him to dismiss her.

Tony took his hands out of his pockets and took a step towards her. Another. His eyes were hungry. 'I didn't want to talk.'

He snaked his arm around her waist and pulled her close.

Mel's mouth dried up as that boiling pit inside erupted and surged through her body, setting every atom alight.

'What I wanted to do. Was. This.'

Tony tugged her closer, so she was hard up against him, lifted her chin and laid his lips upon hers. Soft, tender. Delicious little kisses peppered upon her lips, around the edges, along her jawline.

Was that why he'd been so sullen today? Had need made him cranky? Need for her? Had Tony's feelings for her changed as hers had for him?

Tony walked her backwards towards her old sofa, each kiss deepening, becoming more fevered with every step. Was the lock on the door flicked over? She half wondered as she angled her neck to the side, giving him more access, wanting to feel his lips on every square centimetre of her body.

The soft cushioning of the couch caught her legs and they collapsed, a tangle of legs and arms, a tangle of tongues. His hand skirted under her top, caressing her stomach, sending shivers of desire downwards. She tugged at his T-shirt, lifting it over his head, revealing that incredible chest. Toned, taut, just made for dribbling chocolate sauce and slightly whipped cream onto. Perhaps later.

'Melanie! There's someone here to see you!'

Her mother's voice sent them scattering from the couch like naughty teenagers who'd been caught getting up to things they shouldn't have.

Mel quickly tucked her top back in. 'Oh bugger, I forgot I'd asked a sales rep to pop in. He said it would be sometime this week…'

'Don't worry.' Tony reached for his T-shirt and slipped it over his head, hiding away that which she'd so enjoyed touching seconds before. That which she had some great plans for… 'We can talk later.'

'I like our talks.' She grinned, happy to see Tony smile back at her. All hint of tension gone.

'So do I. A lot. Well, you'd better get going.' He fished his mobile out of his back pocket and looked at the screen. 'And I'd better go open up the pub or the few regulars I have will be after me with pitchforks.'

Valerie popped her head around the door. 'Melanie? There's a man down here who needs to talk to you about hot-chocolate syrups? He's rather good-looking. Make sure you buy them, and be sure to push them on your customers,' she ordered. 'I've far more of a chance with him if he has to restock on a regular basis.' She turned and headed back down to the café.

Mel shook her head in despair. 'It's always about her. Even when she says it's not, it is.'

Tony took her hands in his. 'Have that talk with her. Show her how her actions hurt you. Who knows, instead of running off with a rugby player or salesman, she may see the light, see how amazing you are, and stick around.' He kissed the top of her head and waved goodbye.

Mel bit her lip. Tony was okay with the idea of her mother sticking around for longer, maybe even forever? And would her mother stick around? She had seemed happier in the last couple of days. Didn't moan when asked to do something. She'd even offered to do things in the café. And she kept talking about Mel and Tony's wedding. Was she finally ready to be a real mum?

What about your fake engagement?

The thought jumped up out of nowhere to darken her mood. Stupid deal. She'd figure her way out of that when the time came. She touched her lips, tender from Tony's fervent kisses. Or maybe she wouldn't have to.

CHAPTER NINE

'Are you ready for today?' Tony's deep voice was lower still, heavy with sleep.

Then again, it was early. Earlier than usual – 3.30 a.m.

'I'm ready. I think. I mean, there's not a lot we can do, right? Just play along with the whole engagement party thing and see what happens? Hope no one asks for their gifts back when we break up?'

Tony's teeth flashed in the darkness as he laughed. 'Do we have time for…?'

'No,' Mel sighed. 'I wish. There's too much to do. Maybe later.'

'Although we'll probably fall into bed. Exhausted. And go to sleep. That's what happens to most couples, isn't it?'

'You're thinking of weddings.' Mel reached out and took Tony's hand in hers. 'Most couples get to the end of the big day and go to sleep. But who can blame them? By the time most people get hitched the mystery of each other's bodies is well and truly gone.'

'I don't think I'll ever stop enjoying the mystery of your body.'

'Stop smirking,' she ordered, glad he couldn't see her own smirk, covered up by the blanket she'd hitched up to her nose to keep warm.

'I'm not.'

'And stop trying to sound affronted. Besides, we're only having an engagement party.'

'Which is being preceded by feeding two hungry rugby teams this morning. Then there's the actual rugby game where you'll be serving hot drinks and I'll be serving alcoholic ones. Then there's the after-match function. Then our function.'

The enormity of the day hit Mel. There was so much to do work-wise. Let alone having to lie to the whole town at their engagement party. Pretend to be a happy couple. Pretend to be in love. Although that act was proving far easier than she'd ever have thought. It didn't even feel that much like acting any more....

Mel tossed the blanket aside. 'Well, I guess we'd better get up. Give me a shove out of this infernal bed, would you?'

Tony obliged. 'Your turn,' he said. 'Yank me out of bed?'

Mel laughed and padded over to Tony's side. 'We sound like an old married couple. Like, really old. And this is our morning ritual.' She took Tony's hand and pulled with all her might. 'How did you ever get out of bed without me?'

Then she remembered that infamous reputation of his. Perhaps he rarely ever had to get out on his own? The idea left her cold. Why couldn't he have been a one-girl kind of guy instead of a player? As much fun as she was having, as much as a small part of her hoped it could become something more, something real, she wasn't sure she could ever entirely trust her heart to him. To anyone. Not after she'd been left by her mother every time she'd found a new man, unceremoniously dumped on her grandma's doorstep, only to be picked up whenever Valerie had thought she'd finally met the one and was ready to settle down again. It had been a long, hard lesson about trusting your heart to those you loved, and once she'd escaped that hurtful cycle she'd promised herself one thing – she was never being left by anyone she loved that much ever again. It simply wasn't worth the pain.

Warm lips touched her cool head. 'What's going through that beautiful mind of yours?'

'Nothing important. Do you think we've ordered enough eggs for breakfast?'

'Twelve dozen should do it. It's nice of your mum to run the café while you help me out here this morning.'

'Yeah, she's been so helpful since you forced her to help out. It's so unlike her.' Mel slipped on her jeans and a T-shirt and pushed her feet into her sneakers.

'You sound suspicious.'

'I can't help but be suspicious. Valerie and I have never

spent this much time together. She's never paid this much attention to me, to my life… it's kind of disconcerting.'

'I can imagine.' Tony leant against the wall, his forehead furrowed in thought. 'The only time my father had all his attention on me was the day he died.'

Mel straightened up. Tony didn't talk a lot about his father and yet now he was? Had her revelation prompted one within him?

'He was a good father, though, wasn't he?'

'Kept us fed and watered. But yeah, all his focus was on this place.'

Mel nodded. She'd gathered that much.

'And it was until the day he died. Even his last words… they weren't "I love you, son", just the instruction that this place was to become my one and only priority.'

Mel held her breath, kept herself still. This wasn't a conversation. It was a confessional and Tony had to get something off his chest. One little movement, one distraction, could ruin that for him.

'*Your sister is a big girl, she's got the babies to keep her focused. The Bullion is yours, son. You take care of it. Keep her the same. She's all we have left of her…* And then he was gone.'

Mel licked her lips and paused. 'Isn't this what you've always wanted? You could have gone out into the world. Gone further in school. Been anything you wanted…'

'Yeah. I always wanted to take over The Bullion.' Tony

kicked the heel of his shoe into the wooden floor. 'I'd assumed she'd be mine one day, once Dad was ready to loosen his iron grip on her. I wish he had sooner, let me do more while he was still here. Then maybe I could have figured out ways to make her financially stable. Wouldn't have run this place even further into the ground. If he could see how much worse things have become in the last year...' Tony closed his eyes and shook his head. 'I've really let him down.'

A jolt of irritation hit Mel. 'Tony. Stop that. That pity you're feeling? That self-doubt? Ditch it. Now.'

Tony opened his eyes and faced Mel. They were cool, distant. Stuck in the past.

'You need to realise one thing, Tony, and it's something you've helped show me – the past is the past and going over it doesn't change it. But the future? We're the only ones in control of that. So ask yourself, Tony, what is it you want?'

Tony ran his hand through his curls and sighed. 'To see this place succeed. To make Dad proud. To turn it not into a memorial for my mother, but a living embodiment of her. Spirited. Funny. Embracing. That's really all I ever wanted.'

'And you're doing it. You are. In less than a week you've made huge changes and things are only going to get better. You've always had the ability to make this place a success, Tony McArthur, and it's happening. You're making it happen. But it's not enough to do it just to make your father proud, you need to do it to make *you* proud.'

Tony's eyes cleared, all trace of indecision gone. He moved towards her in the gloom and took her hand. 'Are you ready for today?'

'As much as I can be.'

'As much as *we* can be.' He lifted her hand and kissed it. 'We're in this together, Mel. Till the bitter end.'

And that was the problem. The end would no doubt be bitter. In Mel's experience it always was.

***

Tony tried to catch Mel's eye as he poured an orange juice for one of the local rugby players. Was he imagining things or was she avoiding him? She'd gone quiet that morning. Only talking to him to issue instructions, making sure they were working on separate sides of the kitchen, or he behind the bar and she out in the main room serving up the breakfast to the two teams. She hadn't even laughed at some of the ridiculous taunts being tossed out over the room.

The Big Breakfast had always been his favourite part of grudge-match day. The testosterone-charged room filled with blokes who thought for one day they were every bit as strong and tough as the national rugby team, but in reality were shorter, softer and a whole lot less skilled.

Yet they brought everything they had to the game and it started with trying to mentally knock over the other team with whatever jibes they could come up with.

'The only balls you're any good at playing with are the ones in your pants!' a Rabbits Leap local mouthed off to a Babbler lad.

'Whatever, mate. At least when I'm fumbling balls it's those ones and not the ones on the pitch.'

The men roared with laughter, mouths open, teeth gleaming, half-chewed bacon and eggs threatening to spray all over the table. Who would've thought that right now they'd be elbow to elbow having a great time together, but in a few hours ready to ruck each other to death in order to win the coveted cup. A gold-plated affair that had been travelling between the villages for fifty-three years now.

'Calm down, boys. You're in the presence of a lady and she doesn't need to hear that smut.' Tony raised his eyebrows in warning. 'Tone it down.'

He picked up a couple of empty plates and took them back to the bar where a small stack was waiting to be put into the dishwasher.

'You didn't have to do that, you know.' Mel eyed the stack of plates.

Oh, so Mel was talking to him?

'Do what? Pick up dirty plates? It's no biggie.'

'Not that. I'm talking about telling that lot to calm it

down. I wasn't bothered by it.' She heaved the stack up and balanced them against her chest for support.

'Here, let me take those.' He went to grab them but she stepped backwards.

'I don't need your help, Tony. I can handle a few dirty jokes as well as a few dirty plates.' Her expression was flinty with determination, her face pale.

What was up with her?

'Have I done something wrong?' He went to touch her shoulder, noticed her flinch, and thought better of it. Maybe she'd taken his moment of honesty as weakness and it had disgusted her? After she'd revealed the tragic story of her childhood he'd wanted to share something with her of his in case she'd been feeling awkward about sharing so much with him. He'd meant to tell her about the time he tried to ride a cow and broke his leg but told everyone he'd broken it climbing the biggest tree in the schoolyard, or about the time he'd given his teacher a love note only to be let down gently, but his father's dying wish had come out – and the fear he had that he'd never be good enough. Not only a show of weakness, but no doubt a total turn-off.

'No, Tony, you haven't done anything wrong and that's part of the problem.' She spun round, kicked the kitchen's swinging door open and disappeared inside.

Tony threw his hands up in frustration. Something was definitely up, but he didn't have time to figure it out.

He had to finish watering this lot, clean up the mess and prepare for that afternoon's game.

***

'I'm sorry for being an idiot earlier.' Mel grabbed her coat from Tony's bed and shrugged it on to protect against the icy wind that had blown up during the morning.

'Are you going to tell me what brought it on?' Tony picked up one of his old rugby scarfs and wrapped it around Mel's neck.

Should she? Mel had spent the morning immersed in work while trying to figure out how to handle their situation. Her feelings for Tony were growing, deepening even more after he'd opened up to her that morning. All she'd wanted to do was hold him in her arms and show him how amazing he was, but that would've only made her want him more, so instead she'd lectured him. Then gone cold on him, hoping distance would help harden the way her heart bloomed with joy whenever she saw him. But she couldn't help but sneak looks at him while he was chatting with the players, sharing a joke, looking far too handsome. Each glance weakening her resolve.

The way she saw it, they were going to have to break up at some point soon to save her from the kind of hurt that would take an age to get over, but it had to look real, it had to look right. Most importantly, it had to be in a way that her mother would understand she needed time to lick her wounds, and that meant time alone, not time spent looking for a man to lick her wounds for her.

'Have I wrapped the scarf around your neck too tightly? You don't look like you're breathing.' He dropped his head closer to hers, his hand playfully loosening the knot.

Such a small gesture, a man giving a woman a scarf, but no man had ever done something quite so sweet, so nurturing, for her before. Why did he have to be such a good guy, but such an unattainable one?

'I'm fine. I can breathe. Promise.' Except she couldn't, not when he was standing less than half a foot away, those aquamarine eyes of his sparkling madly, that irresistible scent enveloping her, making her want to step that little bit closer, to remove their layers of clothing, to feel his body moulded against hers…

'Good. Breathing's important at a rugby game. Deep breathing is extra important. You're going to need those lungs of yours for screaming out "Go, the Leap".'

'I've never been to a rugby game before…' Mel admitted.

Tony's mouth dropped open. 'Are you serious?'

'Deadly. When you're being raised between two women there isn't much call for going to games.'

'But your mother loves men. I've seen her ogling the boys. You'd have thought she'd have been to every game going?'

'Her taste ran to the kind of men who you could find in bars. Perhaps because they were easier to lure after a few too many.' The joke fell flat. Not that it was much of a joke to Mel. Or a joke at all.

'You met me at a bar...'

'I think owners of country pubs are a different kettle of fish. Besides, we're not "together" together, you know that.'

His brow crinkled and he straightened up, reaching for his jacket.

'True.' The word was short, sharp. His playfulness gone.

Had she offended him? Said something to upset him? Or was it more than that? Was he also beginning to have feelings for her? Was this becoming as real for him as it was for her?

'Tony?'

'Hmm?' He turned his back on her and rummaged in his wardrobe looking for something.

'Just so we're clear, this is still just a fake relationship, right? Only valid until such time as my mother leaves? I mean, the menu we've created is working. I've seen locals come in for a drink, then return the next night for a drink and a meal. Things are looking up for The Bullion. For you. So it's just my end of the deal that needs to be completed...'

His rummaging stilled. What was he thinking? How

was he feeling? What she'd have given to be able to see his face right now, to read his thoughts! She wasn't exactly putting her feelings for him out there, but she was giving him an opportunity for him to own up to his. If he had any.

Movement. Finally. She watched those large, strong hands of his, hands that had sent her into shrieks of ecstasy she didn't know she was capable of, grasp an olive-coloured hunting hat. He turned to her, his face impassive.

'Yep, fake. We're just two adults making the best of a mad situation, that's all.'

'Okay. Good. Now we're clear.' Mel looked down at her woollen, sock-clad feet and hoped Tony hadn't seen the flash of disappointment her heart had felt. She glanced back up, his face remaining unreadable, yet his body had relaxed a little. The white-knuckle tension with which he'd held his hat had disappeared. So he was relieved? Glad to know he'd be free of her as soon as her mother left? Well, at least she knew where she stood. In the exact place she'd always stood. Alonesville. Population: her. He had a point about making the best of the situation, and as one day she'd end up back in her bed in her small flat all by herself, waiting for the right guy, the guy who would pull her blockade down and see her for who she really was – the guy she'd thought might have been Tony – she may as well enjoy the warm bed and the wrong guy while she could.

Just like her mother would?

She shivered. The last thing she'd ever wanted to become was her mother. Flitting from man to man. Settling for Mr Just Right For Now. But maybe her mother had been on to something. Maybe Mr Just Right For Now was okay, every now and then, so long as you knew where you stood and didn't expect it to become the world's greatest love affair. She took a step towards Tony and reached for his hat. Standing on tiptoes she placed it firmly on his head, inhaling his earthy scent, her body bending towards him. It knew what it wanted, even if neither of them did. He caught her by her hips and held her, his eyes searching hers.

'Are you sure you're clear on what you want?' His words were raspy.

Mel hesitated. She knew the answer he wanted was 'yes'. There was no way he wanted her for the long term. It wasn't in his make-up. Yet some irrational part of her wanted to say 'no', wanted to invite him to be with her, to love her. She nodded. No words were safer than the chance of her voice betraying her true feelings.

'Okay then.' Tony tilted her chin and brought his lips down upon hers. The kiss lingered, long, soft, sweet.

How could something that felt so right be so wrong?

He pulled back. 'We could be late for the rugby, you know?'

Mel tipped her head and raised an eyebrow. 'Late? For

the biggest rugby game of the year? My first rugby game at that? You're pretty to look at, McArthur. But you're not that hot.' She took his hand. 'Come on, lover boy, let's go watch grown men chuck a ball around.'

***

'And that's a knock-on from Simon O'Halloran. Babbler are hurting today. Their grandmothers could play better than this.' The tinny voice of the commentator echoed around the pitch, eliciting laughs from the locals and boos of annoyance from the few Babbler supporters who'd made it to the game.

'Can he say that? Surely there are rules around being rude to the opposition?' Mel looked up at Tony, her face creased in puzzlement.

Her lack of rugby knowledge was so cute, and surprisingly hot. Or maybe that hotness was coming from the way she was snuggled right into him, both arms encircling his waist as she tried to escape the cold wind. A wind that could stick around for as long as it liked as far as Tony was concerned.

'They can say that. They can say anything. It's not an official match like you'd see on TV. And besides, our guy's being nice. I didn't get to the game down in Babbler last year but I heard their commentator got personal, so much so one of the players needed counselling in order to feel like a man again.'

'No.' Mel's eyes widened. 'Surely not?'

'That's what I heard.'

'And why is a knock-on a bad thing? I thought the whole point of the game was to move the ball forward.'

Her lips pouted in confusion. Their bow-shaped pinkness sending his thoughts straight to lust-land.

'Well, it is, but you have to move the ball forward by moving the ball backwards... passing it backwards, I mean.'

'Except for when you kick it?'

He brought her closer against him as she shivered. 'Something like that. Are you enjoying this?'

He knew the answer but he loved seeing her excitement. From the moment they'd arrived she'd joined in the singing and cheering. Booed when the rest of the town had. Hollered encouragement along with everyone else. Bounced up and down against him when the captain of the team had scored a try. Best try ever as far as Tony was concerned, and that had nothing to do with the side-stepping that had occurred on field in order for the try to be scored.

'Have you seen my mum?'

Mel's constant searching of the crowd hadn't gone unnoticed by Tony. Why she thought her mother would come to the game he didn't know, since she'd promised to take care of things in town.

'Isn't she meant to be looking after the café for you?'

'Yeah.' Mel scoured the bleachers once more. 'But I thought she'd skip town and join us. It's not like there's anyone to serve right now. They're all here. Who knew a game of rugby could be such an event?'

'Well, in Rabbits Leap it is. We don't have many events to get excited about. There's this. The Farmer of the Year Awards, which, trust me, isn't anything to look forward to. And the Christmas Parade is good fun, if only because it's a chance to see a tipsy Santa throwing lollies out to the kids and nearly falling off his sleigh.'

A smile lit up Mel's face, twisting his heart. He was going to miss seeing that smile on a regular basis. She smiled often, but that particular smile, her warm, welcoming full-bodied smile... she only let it loose every now and then, and when she did it could warm the coldest of winds. The stoniest of hearts.

Back at the pub he'd been sorely tempted to tell Mel that his feelings were real, that he wanted her. Because they were. And he did. Somewhere, somehow, and at some point in the last few days she'd got under his skin and made a home there. He'd begun to wake up looking forward to seeing that smile of hers. He'd wanted to get up and work next to her at the café, even if it meant doing a hundred dishes. He'd enjoyed feeling her body curl up against his after a long night on their feet at The Bullion, working together in perfect unison, ensuring the customers were well fed, well watered and well happy.

She'd become part of him. But as soon as her mother left, that would be that. They'd end their 'engagement' and go back to being two people who might see each other a couple of times a week when he poured her a glass of wine. Two people who'd exchange pleasantries then go about their business.

Although, after everything they'd shared, could they ever really go back to that? Would Mel want to?

'Go, you good things. Go!' Mel was jumping up and down bellowing with all her might.

Tony turned his attention to the field to see one of the Rabbits Leap players dive over the try line, delivering the team the victory they'd spent the last forty minutes of the second half looking for.

'They won, Tony. They did it.' Her petite face turned up to his, her eyes shining brilliantly, her cheeks rosy with the cold and excitement.

'They did.' He bent his head and kissed her, hard and fast, letting the excitement of the game, the exhilaration of winning, and the thrill of finally understanding what it was to fall for someone take over. Her lips heated up against his as he tasted her, savoured her, revelled in her sweetness, saving it to memory. Her hands snaked up his back and curled round his neck as he pulled her hard up against him, cursing the puffiness of their jackets, a barrier to what he wanted. To feel her against him. Skin on skin.

The crowd around them cheered. This time there was no chant of 'Go, the Leap', it was 'Go, Tony', 'Go, Mel'.

He broke away and gazed at Mel, whose wide-mouth, eyes-lit-up smile was back.

'If that's how you react when the team wins I really think the boys ought to have a break and play again in another couple of minutes. And again. And again.' Mel reached down and slipped her hand into his jeans back pocket.

If any other woman had done that, touched him in such a proprietary manner, he'd have shied away. It was a small gesture to some, but to him it came with a sense of ownership and he'd never wanted to feel owned by any woman ever, until now.

Tony nodded to the players who were trudging wearily off the field. They may have been sporting huge grins but eighty minutes of rugby had taken its toll on their barely trained bodies. 'Doesn't look like you'll be getting your wish…'

Mel mock-sighed. 'Well, I guess I'll just have to remember that one kiss then.'

'We could make this a standing yearly date?' he whispered in her ear.

Mel took a step back and regarded him with guarded eyes and a forced smile. 'Because that would work. The town would understand that. Oh, we're engaged. Oh, we've broken up. Oh, we still like to kiss once a year at the rugby.' The forced smile widened. 'At least it'd give them something to gossip about.'

'Mel, we need to talk. I need to talk...' He reached for her hand but she dodged backwards shaking her head.

'Sorry, Tony. I've got to get going, check on Mum. I'll see you later.'

Tony watched her weave away through the crowd. Her shoulders hunched, head lowered, armour up. It was time he found the courage to say what he really wanted to say, needed to say. To tell Mel how he felt, lay his cards on the table; because, despite all their big talk of this being a deal with a finite time, he suspected she was struggling as much as he was. What they had, what they'd discovered, was too special to let go. Too important to toss out when her mother finally blew out of town. Their engagement party was just a few hours away... he'd do it then. He'd show Mel and Rabbits Leap exactly how much he wanted to be with her.

CHAPTER TEN

'Mum?' Mel let herself in the back door of the café, confusion pulsing in her veins. And not just the confusion she felt about Tony. When he'd kissed her back at the game she could've sworn it was for real. The kind of kiss a man would give a woman he cared for and not a woman he had to pretend he cared for. But this wasn't about him, or her feelings towards him. This was about her mother. She'd tried to call on the way back from the game to make sure everything was okay, but the phone had remained unanswered, going to the answering machine each of the five times she'd called.

'Are you here, Mum?'

The kitchen replied with silence. She hurried through to the café, her gut roiling with an uncomfortable mix of disappointment and desire, only to find it empty. Not just empty, deserted. Locked up. She glanced up at the clock on the wall. It was nowhere near closing time, in fact it was only 1.30. Lunchtime. The café should've been open. There should've been food in the cabinets. There should've been someone behind the counter ready to greet customers.

Instead? Nothing. No neon lights danced around the windowsill announcing the café was open. No warmth hit you in the face as you opened the door into a brightly lit, welcoming room. No sound of a grinder going as a coffee was created. Just dark, ominous stillness.

Her blood ran cold as she reached the top of the stairs and laid her hand upon the door handle. What if something had happened to her mother? What if she'd fallen over and injured herself last night? Been lying on the floor screaming for help until she passed out? What if it were worse than that? Mel sucked back a lungful of air. And another. Whatever she was about to discover she had to be calm, collected. She had to be prepared to deal with the worst. There was no point getting hysterical before she knew the facts. She pushed down on the handle and opened the door slowly.

'Mum?' The word floated through the air, soft, cautious, yet unmistakably heavy with worry.

No answer came.

Mel stepped into the room. 'Valerie?'

It only took a few short steps to reach the door that led to her bedroom and bathroom. She turned the knob and pushed the door open just enough to poke her head in. 'Mum? Are you sick? Can I get you something?'

Still no answer. She peered through the gloom, but

the drawn blinds kept her from seeing anything. Maybe her mother was passed out cold? Maybe it really was something worse? Mel banished the thought. She was just being stupid. Her mother was fine. Probably just tired from all the helping she'd been doing.

Mel pushed the door fully open and ran to the bed. 'Mum. Wake up.' She ran her hands over the covers looking for her mother's form. No body shape appeared. She wasn't there. Then where was she?

Mel turned to the curtains and pulled them open, hoping the early-afternoon sun would shed some light on the situation. The bed had been made haphazardly, as had always been her mother's way. There was a half-empty glass of water on the bedside table. But no jewellery. No skincare either. Odd.

Mel stepped through into the bathroom. No cosmetics. No toothpaste. No toothbrush. She sniffed the air. Her mother's musky sweet perfume had gone as well.

Unable to believe what she was seeing, Mel moved back into the bedroom and looked under the bed. No suitcase. Maybe she'd moved it underneath the sofa? She headed back to the lounge and saw a note folded in half, placed in the middle of the coffee table, her name in large, perfect cursive written on top.

'Mel, I've gone on a road trip with Phillip. He's as sweet as his hot chocolate! Have a good time at your engagement party. Valerie.'

She'd gone. Mel's breath caught in her throat as a slow ache formed in her heart. Valerie had taken off, again. Without a single thought for how Mel would feel. As usual.

Mel collapsed on the ground and curled into a ball. Tears that had risen when she'd thought her mother was sick or worse now spilt, but these tears were hot with anger. And humiliation. She'd been stupid to hope her mother might be around for longer, that there was a chance they could repair their relationship. She should know by now that people don't stick around, that the people you love just leave. What an idiot she'd been to let her guard down, to open her heart, to believe she was worthy of love.

If her own mother couldn't love her, then how could Tony?

Mel pressed her forehead into the cold floorboards and took a deep breath, held it, slowly exhaled. Breathing out the last of her tears. She'd cried enough for her mother. It was time to get over it. To get over her. To move on. But first she had to end things with Tony before she fell for him even further.

She heaved herself up and trudged into her room. Not her mother's room. Not Tony's room. Hers. Her space, her place, her haven. She caught a glimpse of herself in the mirror that hung above her dresser. She was a wreck. Hair unkempt, eyes rimmed red from those wasted tears, her light dusting of make-up all but blown off by the wind. She shook her head. Whoever had been invited to her engagement party would expect her to turn up to the pub a bit glammed-up but they could deal with their disappointment. This was who she was. Melanie Sullivan, the unwashed, unlovable girl who'd never let anyone break her heart again.

She curled her hair behind her ears, and tried not to think about how Tony had done the very same thing after they'd made love the previous night. So he could see her beautiful face better, he'd told her, his voice warm with intimacy – no wonder the women of the town still liked him after he'd loved and left them. He made a woman feel special, made her believe he truly cared. But Mel was no fool. There was no chance she and Tony would ever work. He'd get bored of her like her mother had and eventually he'd leave. No. Breaking things off now was the only way, and at least with her mother gone it was going to be easy to do. Their deal was done. She could thank her mother for that at least.

**

'I just want to say thanks to Rabbits Leap for hosting us. Cheers to you.' The captain of the Bad Boys of Babbler raised his pint glass in the direction of the townsfolk who'd populated The Bullion for the post-match drinks and awards ceremony. 'And to you, Tony. You're a good man for having us again. I'd like to say that I hope we haven't done too much damage, but let's be honest, considering the state of this place, you'd never know.'

The town tittered at the light-hearted joke. As for Tony? Not so much. He clenched his fists, glad they were hidden away beneath the bar where no one could see how much the banter had hit home. Yeah, the place was rundown, but it had been a good week. Mel's menu had been a hit. The takings had been above and beyond what he'd projected and he now had plans to turn things around further. He'd have to talk to a bank manager, though, because it'd mean getting a loan, something he'd sworn he'd never do. His father had always said a strong man relied on no one but himself, but after the last week, where Tony had found himself coming to rely… more than rely… coming to *need* Mel's help, he'd realised a strong man knew when to ask others to give him a hand and there was no shame in borrowing money if it meant bigger and better things, greater returns and the potential for huge success. And he meant to make The Bullion the biggest success story around. A place loved by others as much as he loved her, as much as his father had. She deserved nothing less. His mother's memory would remain. And the first thing he'd do was unpack her photos from the box in the attic, photos of her with his dad, with Jody and himself, photos of them all together, and place them around the bar.

'You may have beaten us this year, Rabbits Leap, but

you'll be heading our way next year and we'll be ready.' The captain raised his glass in the air one more time, beer sloshing over the sides onto the threadbare carpet.

Tony shook his head. To think he would've cringed at the sight of that a week ago, at the thought of the cleaning bill a few nights of beer swilling rugby players had caused, but tonight it didn't matter because next week that carpet wouldn't be there.

A rousing chorus of 'Here Comes the Bride' interrupted his thoughts. He glanced up to see Mel standing inside the door, her body arrow-straight, chin held high, and that smile, the one that never reached her eyes, plastered on her face. Yet those eyes, they held more sorrow than usual. Something was up. More than that... something was off. She seemed smaller than usual. Paler. Yet that undercurrent of determination she carried with her was still there.

Her eyes met his as she wove through the crowds towards him, avoiding elbows and feet with a dainty dexterity.

She reached him unscathed, although those narrowed eyes, rimmed in red and a touch puffy, kept shifting about the room like a wild animal ready to escape at the first sign of danger.

'Are you okay?' He took her hands in his and pulled her in towards him, hoping his touch would help soothe whatever wound it was she was carrying.

His gesture was met with rigidity. She didn't budge from her spot. Didn't meld into him. Wouldn't allow him to comfort her.

'You and I need to talk.' She gazed at a point just to the left of his ear.

Tony's stomach clenched. This wasn't good. 'You and I need to talk' was never followed by a good conversation. He'd used those very same words often enough to know. What had gone wrong? Had he done something to annoy her? To make her so angry her hands were shaking in his right this minute?

'Ladies and gentlemen, thank you for coming to such an auspicious event.' Tony closed his eyes. Talk about bad timing. Tom Brown, the town's unofficial spokesperson and owner of the stationery shop, which also produced the weekly newspaper, had taken the microphone. There would be no conversation between Mel and himself, not while Tom had the floor. 'Let's be honest, the rugby game was good and all, and winning is always a fine thing, but tonight we join together to celebrate the beginning of a union we never expected.'

The crowd cheered and turned to Mel and Tony. Yep. They well and truly weren't having any talk about anything any time soon. Mel's jaw was set and her skin had taken on a green tinge. He wondered if she saw the same green tinge in his own skin, because he wasn't feeling all that good right about now. His previous ebullience at finally deciding to take some big steps within his business and within his personal life had left the building.

'Let's be honest, Tony. You've been known around these parts as a confirmed bachelor. A ladies' man. Some have gone so far as to say that you're the embodiment of Rabbits Leap because you make like a rabbit then leap onto the next thing...'

The crowd whooped at the joke. Tony closed his eyes, but not before seeing Mel's nostrils flare in disapproval.

'But it seems you've proven us all wrong by finding yourself a good woman. Mel, you've not been in town all that long. Let's be honest, you won't be considered a full-blown local until you've been here another forty-nine years, but by marrying one of our favourite sons we're pretty sure we can halve the fifty-year rule and call you a local in another twenty-four. Now I'm sure you'd like to listen to me yammer on about this all night, but how about we get those two lovebirds up here on the stage and show them how happy we are for them.'

Tony took a deep breath and opened his eyes to see Mel shaking her head subtly and mouthing 'no'. Tony shrugged. What could he do? The people around him were a force to be reckoned with at the best of times, but with a rugby win and a few pints in their bellies they were unstoppable. Hands were already pulling at his shirt, pushing Mel and him up towards the makeshift stage, inch by heel-dragged inch.

'There they are! Get on up here and say a few words.'

Tom pressed the microphone into Tony's hands, and then leant in for a quick hug and slap on the back. 'Your dad would have been mighty proud of you, son,' he muttered gruffly into his ear.

Tony pulled away and nodded his thanks, while trying to ignore the sheen of wetness in the eyes of the man who'd been his father's best mate. He hoped that his dad would have been proud of him, but he didn't know that he would've been. His father had never liked liars. People who deceived others. He was the kind of guy who shot straight from the hip and never told a story that wasn't true. A couple of rules Tony had done his best to live his life by until he got into this thing with Mel. Sure, he'd got into it in order to better The Bullion, but they'd been living a lie. Pulling the wool over the eyes of the town he loved. He knew that if his dad was looking down on him right now he'd have his arms crossed, his brow furrowed, and he'd be shaking his head in disapproval.

Or maybe he wouldn't be, because, if Tony were honest with himself, he didn't feel like he was living a lie. Not any more. Somehow, at some point, he'd begun to love the woman next to him. Loved her determination. Loved her spark. Loved how she gave everything all she had while still making time to help others. He couldn't imagine spending a night away from her. Mel had come to mean as much to him as The Bullion. And who knew, if his dad was able to see him right here and right now, maybe he'd see that, too. Maybe he would be proud, after all.

And maybe it was time he manned up and told the person who needed to know it most how he felt about them.

His quivering hands stilled with resolution as he brought the microphone up to his lips. 'Evening, everyone.'

The crowd hollered 'evening' back at him.

'Thanks for coming tonight. Congrats on your win, boys. Knew you could do it. Not sure how you managed it after eating me and two towns over out of bacon and eggs this morning, but then I did see how much beer the opposition drank in the last few days...'

Laughter filled the pub as a few of the opposition made rude gestures at Tony as they drained their glasses to make a point.

'It's been a crazy few days here at The Bullion, but I couldn't have done it without the help of this truly amazing woman standing next to me.' He snaked his arm around Mel's waist and tried to pull her closer but his touch was met with resistance. He glanced down to see her staring out at the horde that had come to celebrate their engagement. A tiny vein pulsed at her temple. That jaw of hers looked like it would be locked into position forever if she didn't loosen it up soon. Then there were her eyes. Red-rimmed, their velvety chocolate hue shadowed in pain. What was going on with her? Maybe his speech would help, could make things better.

'I can say that, without a doubt, Mel is the best thing to have come into my life, ever. I only wish I'd let her in a bit earlier. In the last while she has taught me what it means to take risks. To think outside my own small world. She's shown me the past doesn't have to rule my future. That change can be a good thing. A great thing. Thanks to Mel I have some big changes coming up for this place, for me...'

Mel turned towards him. Her eyes were narrowed, her brow furrowed, her pixie face tight, closed.

'...and I look forward to having her with me every step of the way.'

The gathering roared their approval, stamping feet and clapping hands.

'Speech. Speech. Speech. Speech.' Their chant began soft and low, stepping up in force with each word, demanding Mel share her side of the story. Tony went to hand her the microphone. Her hand blocked him, taking him by the wrist. She gave a tiny shake of her head and mouthed 'no'.

'No' what? he wondered. 'No' she didn't want to do a speech. But it wasn't fear he saw in the stoniness of her face. It was determination. So what was that 'no'? A 'no, I can't continue on with this charade'. A 'no, I don't want to be with you every step of the way'. A 'no, I don't want you'. Surely not? Not after the nights they'd spent with each other. Talking. Laughing. Making plans. Making love. It had started off as a bit of a fun, mutual attraction brought to realisation, but the last couple of nights they'd felt like... a couple. He'd thought, despite their mutual denials, that she'd felt it too.

He flicked the microphone's switch onto off and lowered his head. 'Mel, what's wrong? You've seemed off since you got here.'

'I can't do this.' The words were strangled, but clear.

'Well, public speaking isn't for everyone. I can say thanks on your behalf if you want. They'll understand. It wouldn't be the first time.'

'No. Tony. I can't do *this*.'

The flicker of hope Tony had allowed himself to feel blew out. She wasn't talking about speaking into a stupid microphone, or pretending to be engaged while they figured out just what they meant to each other. She was talking about him, her, The Bullion, everything. She couldn't do any of it.

'But, Mel, I thought...' He reached for her hand and tried to ignore the crowd who'd stilled as they realised they were watching drama unfurl upon the stage.

'It doesn't matter what you thought. Nothing matters. I'm done. I'm out. Can you just... I don't know... tell them...' She jerked her head in the direction of the crowd. 'Tell them I'm sorry. And Tony, I really am sorry. More than you'll ever know.'

She ripped her hand from his and fled down the stairs, pushed open the heavy old door as if it were made of polystyrene and disappeared into the night.

Tony ran his hand through his hair. What had just happened? Had Mel really left? And the way she was talking? It sounded like she wasn't just leaving him, she was also leaving the town. He closed his eyes to block the loud whispers of gossiping residents rising up around him. Surely she wouldn't leave the Leap? She loved it here, and all that talk about security and settling down? To tear herself away from the place she'd chosen to call home? Whatever this was it couldn't just be about him and her, not the way things were going. Something had happened between the rugby game and this evening and he had to find out what.

He charged off the stage, thrust the microphone blindly at whoever was closest and ran out the door. Mel could run, but she only had one place to hide and he was going to get to her before she left that. Left him.

He heaved in lungfuls of the cool night air, his arms and legs pumping as fast as his heart, each stride, each breath matched with one word beating through his mind. *Mel.* The storefronts whizzed past, the only sign of life in town was his reflection in their windows, lit by the orange lamps, a glowing force to be reckoned with.

He reached Mel's in minutes. Tony stopped short outside the door, unsure of himself. What should he do? Barge up there and tell her how he felt? Demand she love him back? What if she wouldn't? What if she didn't? Then what? He'd have to go back to The Bullion and tell everyone she'd left him and it was over. The shortest engagement ever.

Would they laugh? Would they think it amusing that the town playboy had got a taste of his own medicine? That the man so many women had declared feelings for had finally had his own feelings hurt? Hurt? If Mel said no, his feelings would be destroyed.

He turned his head up to the flat above to see a shadow pass behind the curtains. She was up there. All he had to do was walk in, walk up and ask her to walk with him forever.

He stepped up to the door, tugged the handle down and pulled.

Ting-a-ling.

She hadn't locked it. Maybe Mel had hoped he'd come? He manoeuvred past the tables and chairs, lifted the counter-top and slipped out back to the kitchen and climbed the stairs. With each step he tried to think, tried to figure out how you went about telling a woman you loved her. Were in love with her. His heart burned hot in his chest, and not from the physical exertion of getting here. He loved Mel. More than anything. And it was the best damn feeling he'd ever had. Better than seeing The Bullion humming with happy punters. Better than the first moment he'd held his nephews in his arms. Better than anything.

'Come in, Tony.'

Mel's voice drifted through the wooden door. She sounded as tired as she'd looked back at the pub.

He turned the knob and opened the door, slowly so as not to frighten her. Not to put her on edge any more than she already was.

'Hey, Mel. How are you?'

She was curled up on her couch, tight, a small ball of black. Her face hidden in her knees. How was she? Obviously not great.

He crossed the room and sat next to her. Should he put his arm around her? Bring her to him? Would she want his touch?

'I'm so sorry about before.' Mel lifted her head. 'I shouldn't have left you like that, but I just... I couldn't go on lying to everyone. Lying to myself.'

Tony lay his hand on her knee, felt its dampness. What had happened to make her this upset? 'But were you lying, Mel? Did you really not want to be with me?'

She tipped her head, her eyebrows drawing together in bafflement. 'I don't know what you mean.'

Tony took a breath. Here goes, fella. This is the rest of your life you're putting on the line. Don't stuff it up. 'It's just... I thought... I felt... perhaps there might have been something more going on between us. You know what I mean?'

Mel shook her head, frown lines appearing on her forehead. 'We were having a good time, making the best of a weird situation...'

'There was that. But more than that. The thing is, Mel… I think you're amazing. Beyond amazing. In all of my life I've never met any woman, *anyone*, like you. You're the strongest person I know. You don't let anyone get in your way, anyone stop you. You work harder than any farmer around here, but don't tell them that or they'll start leaving cowpats on the pub's door.'

A small smile appeared on Mel's lips. Good. He had a chance. He reached for her hand. She let him hold it, her dainty fingers curled around his.

'Without you I would be stuck in a rundown pub, stuck in a rut, chasing my tail while trying to keep all my balls in the air. You've changed that, Mel. You've changed me. The Bullion has been my life, she'll always be my life. But I always thought there was room for only one woman in my heart, and now you've made me realise there's enough room for two. More than enough. The thing is… I… I lo…'

'Don't say it.' Mel wrenched her hand from Tony's and sprung up off the couch.

He watched as she paced up and down the room, shooting furtive glances at the lounge door. Preparing to bolt again?

Tony clamped his hands on his knees. If he got up after her, she'd run. 'Why can't I say how I feel? Why can't I tell the truth?'

'Because the truth is that if you say what you're going

to say, you'll only end up wishing you'd never said it. Besides, that word means nothing. I've heard that word over and over again and then I've been left. The person may have stayed with me for a time, but emotionally they were gone. That word only means something if you plan to stick around. And you're not the sticking-around type, Tony. You've never been that kind of guy. And I'm not the kind of person worth sticking around for. I know that. I'd hoped maybe one day I'd be worth it, but I'm not.'

It didn't take a genius to figure out this wasn't about him, it was about her mother, her past.

'Please, Mel, we have to move on from the past, you said it yourself. What happened to us making our own future?' He rose slowly and held his hand out for her.

'This isn't about the past. It's about learning from your mistakes and I know better than to trust someone, to let myself think they actually care. It only ends up with me being left alone.'

'But I don't want to leave you alone. You have to believe that. I'm not like *her*. I'm not the flighty type.'

Mel laughed. Short, sharp. Bitter.

'Are you sure?' Her eyes narrowed in determination.

Tony's heart sank. He knew what was coming next. His whole life had been the ammunition she was looking for to prove to herself he wouldn't stick with her.

'The thing is, Tony...' She took a step closer to him and raised her finger in accusation. 'You are the flighty type.

That's what you do. You've never settled down. Never even had a girlfriend. You can't stay with just one person. One woman. You might think you can. But you've never managed to do it before and I don't see how you suddenly think you can do it now.'

Exasperation fizzed in Tony's veins. Yeah, she had a point. He'd never been a boyfriend kind of guy, but he'd never met anyone he could see himself sharing his life with. Until now.

'Would I leave? Really? You've seen how I am with The Bullion. Some would say she's a lost cause. But not me. I've stuck with her through thick and thin. Through recessions, through droughts. Even recently, when things were looking more dire than ever, I dug my heels in. Yet you think I couldn't do that with another person? Once I make my mind up about something, someone, I'm all in. I won't budge.'

Mel raised an eyebrow and took a step towards him. 'I don't believe you. Yes, you are all in with The Bullion. But that's because that's who you love. You call her "she". That's your commitment right there. You wouldn't have time to put work into a relationship. The moment things got tough you would bottle it. You'd let things fall apart, just like you did with the pub. If I hadn't come along when I had, you'd have been shutting those doors for good in a few months. You needed me.'

Tony rubbed the back of his neck, frustrated. Mel

didn't want to listen. Refused to. 'Why won't you let me in?' The words were raspy with emotion. He'd never put himself out there like this before, never worn his heart on his sleeve, and here she was making him regret even trying.

Mel stepped towards him, her eyes serious, sad. 'Because you could never let me in. The pub would always be your priority. I know that. I understand that. But I can't accept that. Just once, I want to be someone's priority. Just once.'

'I'm not your mother, Mel…' Tony glanced around the room and realised there was no sign of Valerie. 'Speaking of which, where is she?'

'She's gone. Again. As always. Not even a proper goodbye.' Her words were bitter, harsh. Her eyes heavy with sadness.

Tony raised his hand to caress her cheek. Hoping the touch would somehow show her how much he needed her, how much he was willing to make her his priority, how much he was nothing like her mother. Mel avoided his touch, turned to the door and opened it for him.

'Thanks for being my fiancé, Tony. But I think it's better for both of us if we end things now.'

Tony knew he was meant to leave, but hesitated. Perhaps he could try and explain his feelings one more time, but the frown line running between her eyebrows and the thin arms hugging her body tight told him he'd be wasting his breath. She'd decided their fate. He'd have to accept it. Or at the very least, pretend to. He nodded. And left. Taking a lead-weighted heart with him.

CHAPTER ELEVEN

The sunny yellow walls of her lounge seemed muted. The colourful rugs on the floor dull. Was it time to redecorate?

Mel rolled onto her back and stared at the ceiling, speckled white with gold tips on the stalactite-type formations. It reminded her of the room she'd stayed in at her grandmother's house. Her safe haven from the ever-changing craziness of her mother's life. She'd tried to recreate the same feel here and it had worked, for a while. Lately? Not so much. Since Tony had lost his mind and decided to try and declare his love for her, since she'd shown him the door, everything had felt wrong. For the first time in her life as a business owner, she hadn't opened the doors. Kept the blinds down. The sign on the door turned to 'closed'. Her phone had rung a few times, no doubt the locals wondering when they'd be able to get their freshly baked muffin or a decent cup of coffee, but as the week had gone on, the calls had become fewer and farther between until they'd stopped altogether. Unlike her mobile phone. That had been resolutely blank, not once pinging or ringing to tell her a text or call had come through. Not that she hadn't checked it a hundred times a day, some self-destructive part of her hoping that Tony would call or text, that he'd attempt to change her mind.

But could he?

Mel closed her eyes and shook her head. No. To listen to him, to go to him, to believe that he could and would love her would be a mistake. Not because he didn't love her. She knew he did, could see it in his eyes. He wanted her as much as she wanted him, but there was no way it could last. Not with his reputation. She'd had enough of being dumped for a lifetime. It was never going to happen again.

Her stomach rumbled. A protest against the lack of food she'd been feeding it.

'I know. I'm horrible.' She patted her stomach.

It squeaked its agreement.

'Shall I do something about that then?'

Hauling her tired body up off the couch, Mel made her way down the dark staircase and into the café's kitchen. Maybe cooking would soothe her, rebalance her, as it had always done in the past.

Scones with lashings of butter and dollops of jam. That's what she needed. It had been her grandmother's go-to recipe whenever Mel had landed on her doorstep. Light, fluffy, and a touch magic. One bite and she'd always felt a little bit better about everything.

She pulled out the self-raising flour and salt from the cupboard and grabbed some lemonade and cream from the fridge, switched on the oven to preheat, then set about pouring in the ingredients and folding them through, enough to combine, not enough to leave them tough as nails. The dough quickly came together and it wasn't long before they were ready to be shaped and cut. She sliced a knife through the dough, took the soft squares of heaven and laid them upon a tray.

Now to let the heat do its work.

She went to place the scones in the oven but was interrupted by a knock at the back door. She pulled the curtain back to see who it could be. No. Surely not.

Mel planted her feet hip-wide apart to steady herself, her hands placed on her hips – her fighting stance – and opened the door. 'Mother.'

'Darling! I thought I'd find you back here. Why's the café closed? Are you ill? Shall I call a doctor?' Valerie breezed past Mel and switched the kettle on. 'Oh, I could do with a cup of tea. Make me one? And pop those scones in the oven, won't you, love? I'm famished.'

'No.' The word was low but tough. Tough enough for Valerie to stop her twittering and pay attention. Her mother had been getting away with bad behaviour for far too long. Tony was right; it was time they talked. But first she needed to vent

'No? Well, I guess I could put them in myself. But I'm ever so tired.'

'No, mother. You're not getting scones. Or tea. Or anything from me ever again. I'm done.'

'Done? With what?'

'With you thinking you can flitter in and out of my life whenever you're finished with a man or whenever they're finished with you.' Her anger flared hotter as her mother pursed her lips, not a hint of contrition on her face.

'Melanie, I do not appreciate the tone you're taking with me.' Valerie crossed her arms and looked away. 'And I am allowed to try and find happiness, you know.'

'Happiness? Really? Is that what you've called this life you've led? A search for happiness?' Mel tipped her head and stared at the ceiling, trying to contain her exasperation. 'God, it really has always been about you, hasn't it? What does Valerie want? What does Valerie need? What makes Valerie happy? Want to know the answer to that? Don't worry, I'm not waiting for an answer. I'll tell you. Whatever Valerie pleases. That's what. Just once, couldn't you think of someone other than yourself? Couldn't you just think about me? Care about my needs. My wants.' Mel ran her hands through her hair. 'God, Mother. When will you get tired of making the same mistakes? When will you stop making men the priority and...'

'And what? Make you the priority?' Valerie's back was ramrod-straight, her tone iron-hard. 'What did you think

I did my whole life? I tried to find us a home. Make us a family.'

'But we were a family, Mother. You and me. And Gran when she was with us. Those men? None of them were family. Some weren't as horrible as others. But you'd have been better off without them, especially without the ones that showed as much interest in your daughter as they did in you.'

Valerie's face blanched. Her shoulders buckled. 'I left the moment he tried to touch you.'

'You should have left the moment I asked you to.' Mel's hands curled into fists as she struggled to keep her voice even, as she tried not to let the memories carry her away in a flood of anger. 'The moment he started trying to look at me. The moment he let his hand linger on my knee one second longer than necessary.'

Valerie sank onto the kitchen floor, pulled her knees up to her chest and dropped her head down. 'I just wanted to be loved. I thought he did. I thought they all did.'

The words were muffled, but there was no denying the pain in them.

Mel sank next to her and wrapped her arm around her mother's shaking shoulders. 'I loved you. But I wasn't enough, was I?' Mel whispered.

'You should've been.' The words were ragged, strangled. Valerie looked up at Mel, her damp eyes filled with regret. 'I was a fool. It's just... I saw my mother spend her years alone, raising me without a man. I saw all the families around me, happy, laughing, together, and I swore I would have that one day.'

'But Gran was happy. She loved her life.'

'I didn't see that. I refused to. All I wanted was a father.'

'So that's what you set out to get for me…'

It all made sense. Her mother's constant search for a life partner. The willingness to take on anyone who showed so much as a little bit of interest in her, in Mel. Even when that interest wasn't always healthy.

'I will never forgive myself for letting that arsehole touch you. For getting anywhere near that close to you.'

'I'm just glad you came home when you did.' Mel flashed back to that horrible night. Her mother's husband reeking of beer, his meaty hands hovering over her as she huddled in the corner of her room begging him to go away, to leave her alone.

'So am I, baby girl, so am I…' Valerie curled into Mel, her thin arms bringing her into an embrace.

'I won't ever let another man hurt you ever again.'

'I know you won't.'

'And if Tony happens to even give you one iota of pain, I will have his balls and I will dangle them from the town flagpole. You know, I thought you'd be single like your grandmother forever, too. Happier with your own company than a man's.'

Mel glanced down, not wanting her mother to see the guilt in her eyes. 'Well, I guess things can change.'

'And people can change, too.'

'Can they?' Mel wasn't so sure. She couldn't see Tony giving up his bachelor lifestyle for a family and a white picket fence.

'I hope to.'

'Really?' Mel pursed her lips in disbelief.

'I think it's time I sorted myself out. I was on the road with Phillip, and it didn't feel right. I felt I was in the wrong place. I was missing something. Someone.'

Mel sighed. 'Don't tell me… the guy from Babbler? Well, you've missed him, he's left.'

Valerie patted Mel's knee. 'No. Someone more important. You see, Mel, I do believe I'm done with all the moving, all the men. I've decided it's time I got to know the real love of my life.'

The real love of her life? What was her mother on about?

'I'm talking about you, Mel. All these years of being your mother and I feel like I don't even know you. I want to discover everything there is to know about my daughter. And I'll stay as long as I have to to do it. If you'll have me. If you can find room in your life, with the café, the pub and Tony, to fit me in…'

Mel tried to find the words to tell her mother that the engagement was over.

'He's a good man, that Tony. I don't remember Dad all that well, but Tony has his smile, his kind nature. You've picked a good man. You'll be happy like they were. I know it.'

Mel held her index fingers up to her lids, as tears threatened to flow. Her mother believed Mel had found the kind of love her own parents had. Was she right? Did she see something in Tony that Mel couldn't? Wouldn't. That she refused to see. Could Tony be the kind of man that stuck around? Did it matter now after the way she'd cruelly rejected him? And even if he had changed, could she be the kind of woman who allowed herself to be loved? She glanced down at her black top and jeans. Her armour, as Tony had so rightfully put it. A lock of pink hair flopped down.

An image arose of the girl she'd been before she'd been shunted from home to home, town to town, placed at times in dangerous situations. The girl who'd disappeared as she transformed herself into the kind of woman who kept others at arm's length, who'd smiled but never with her whole soul, who'd laughed but never laughed the brightest. Could she be that kind of person again?

There was only one way to find out.

***

'You owe me one, Tony. You owe me two. Three, even.' Jody set the roller brush in its tray and shook her wrist.

When Tony had called and explained his plan she'd rushed straight over and spent every hour the boys were in school giving him a hand. She'd even broken her limited-screen-time rule when they were around, allowing them more than their allotted time of video games so she could help out some more, much to their delight.

'I owe you everything, Jodes. You've been a trooper.' Tony stretched and surveyed their work. The old place had never looked better. Who knew heartbreak could be the great instigator of change?

'Dad would be proud, you know?'

'I dunno, he loved that carpet. Can you believe underneath those awful paisley swirls lay all that beautiful oak?'

Jody laughed. 'He probably didn't want to ruin it. Probably thought carpet would be the better option. Easier to clean, too. Just let it soak up the beer rather than mop it up. Anyway, it's your pub now – you can do whatever you want to it, whatever makes you happiest. And you are happy, aren't you?' Jody gave him a shrewd look.

He hadn't gone into the details of what had happened between him and Mel, but Jodes knew things had gone south at the engagement party. The whole village had spoken of nothing else for the past week. How Mel had run out, how Tony had come back and thrown all the revellers out. How the café had closed, followed by the pub. Gossip swirled that Tony had done the dirty on Mel, that Mel had never got over the vet she'd been seeing and dumped Tony when she'd figured out she'd been on the rebound. A few locals who'd met Valerie had speculated she'd had something to do with it. Nobody had bothered to ask him what the deal was, of course – not that he'd have told them anyway. As far as he was concerned, there were things to be sorted and changes to be made and that left no time to deal with town chit-chat.

'So, do you think she'll like it?' Tony glanced around the space. It looked lighter, felt brighter. Ready for a new start. A bit like him, really.

'If she doesn't, I'm going to take whatever leftover paint we have, give the boys a couple of brushes and set them loose in her café.'

'Would it matter? It's not like it's been open. You're sure she's still in town?'

Jody nodded. 'According to my two wee spies there's been a light spotted upstairs. "Turns off and on at random times," they said, so I guess that means she didn't scarper without flicking off a light. My question is, how are you going to get her here?'

Tony shrugged. 'I've been wondering about that myself. She was so determined to have nothing to do with me I can't see a simple text asking her to come working…'

'Who would've thought it?' Jody shook her head back and forth slowly in amazement. 'Who'd have thought we'd see the day when Tony McArthur would fall ugly head over big fat heels for a woman?'

Tony rolled his eyes. 'Sure as hell not me. I was determined to love The Bullion and nothing else, to make it a success, to keep Dad's memory alive...'

'Well, if everything goes to plan you'll be doing just that. You'll be keeping Mum's memory alive, too...'

'You think she'd have liked this?'

'She'd have loved it.' Jody ran her hand over the newly re-covered chairs. 'It would have been right up her alley. She'd have loved Mel, too, I reckon.'

'I wish they could have seen it.' The muscles in Tony's throat tightened with emotion. He'd spent so long treading water, trying to keep his little patch of home going, he'd never thought he could make it even better, even more of a home, but he had.

'Me, too, Tony. Me, too.' Jody swiped a tear away. 'Right, there's no point crying over spilt milk and it's just about tea time... Boys!' she yelled, grabbing the broom and using it to thump the ceiling. 'Get your bums down here, it's time to go.' They waited for the elephantine sound of young boys' feet on floorboards. Jody thumped the ceiling with the broom again in warning. 'Three... Two...'

'Coming, Mum,' the boys sang as they scuttled across the room and down the stairs.

'You've got them well trained,' Tony observed.

'Well, it's just me so I have to, otherwise I'd be run ragged.'

'If I can meet someone…' Tony raised an eyebrow.

'Not until they're well older. And by then I'll be so old and haggard from loving and looking after them, no one would want me anyway.'

'Well, there's a daft statement if ever I heard one.'

'What's a daft statement, Uncle Tony?' Jordan called out as the boys crashed into the room, elbowing each other in an effort to be first through the door.

Tony laughed. 'It means your mum needs to listen to her wise younger brother instead of being silly. Now you two get home and be good for your mum, or no more crisps.'

'Yes, Uncle Tony.' The boys nodded, gave each other another elbow and raced out into the street to where Jody's battered old mini was parked.

'Good luck.' Jody leant in and gave Tony a quick hug.

'Thanks, sis. I'm going to need it.'

'If she knows what's good for her, you'll be fine. Call me.'

Jody heaved open the door and stepped out into the sunshine, the door thunking shut behind her, leaving Tony alone. Though hopefully not for too much longer.

***

Mel opened her wardrobe and gazed at her collection of vintage dresses. They'd been her secret pleasure for years.

Countless hours had been spent scouring second-hand stores and online websites looking for pieces that took her fancy. Not that she'd ever worn them. To her they'd always been more like art, something to have sitting there, to admire every now and then, but never to actually use. To wear one would be akin to drawing on a Picasso. At least, that's how she'd justified not wearing them while continuing to wear her plain, black, skinny jeans and colourless tops. Not any more, though. It was time to embrace a life full of colour. To not let her past darken her future.

She sorted through the collection until she found a bright red and yellow, polka-dotted, halter dress with a flared skirt. The first she'd ever bought, at the age of sixteen, from a Call Lane vintage shop. It had cost a good chunk of her first pay cheque, but she'd wanted to buy something to celebrate her new job, her new life, her freedom from her mother. Not that she'd worn it. While it had looked a million dollars on, accentuating her small waist, clinging to her small curves, she'd never put it on outside of her bedroom, the memory of her mother's latest husband's leering eyes sending it straight to the back of her closet. But that was a decade ago and she wasn't that determined yet terrified little girl any more. Tony had made her see that, shown her she was strong, given her the opportunity to prove it to herself. Now she was a grown woman, with her own business and a place she had chosen to make her home, a place she had no intention of leaving.

Mel slipped the dress over her head, the swish of the flared skirt's cool, stiff cotton sending a thrill through her. It was a new day. She'd been baking since four in the morning and it was time to start her life fresh. She tied the thick straps of the halter neck together, put on a baby-pink angora cardigan, and spun round in front of her dress mirror. Ducking down, she rifled through the bottom of the closet for a pair of kitten heels and slid her feet into them. A quick glance at the clock showed it was 6.55 a.m. Go time. Mel gulped and stole another look at her reflection. Bright dress, heels, and her new hair. New hair? More like her natural hair, hidden away along with her natural style for far too long. How would the town take it? Would Tony hear about her new look? Would he care? Care enough to satisfy his curiosity and come find her? Would he like what he saw? A thrill of anticipation raced down her spine. Only time would tell, but first she had a café to reopen and a life to being anew.

Mel half-walked, half-skipped down the stairs, through the kitchen, twirling as her mother wolf-whistled while rustling up a batch of muffins, and made her way through to the café. Flicking the nib on the door, she turned the sign from 'closed' to 'open', sat on the couch and waited for the customers to come.

One hour later she was still waiting. She'd leafed

through the selection of vintage magazines she kept for customers to read while waiting for takeaway coffees half a dozen times. Her eyes flicking up to the clock every minute or so. Where were they? Usually by eight in the morning at least four of her regulars would've popped in during their daily dog walking, and a lorry driver or two would've pulled up as they travelled between towns. Even on her opening day she'd had customers by now. What was going on? Had they thought she'd packed up and left? Had the whole town bought themselves coffee machines for their homes? Had her week of mooning about done her out of a living?

She saw movement on the street out of the corner of her eye. People were still out and about. Good. That ruled out a zombie apocalypse. So where were they going? There was one way to find out.

Standing, Mel opened the door, peaked her head out to see which direction the person she intended to stalk was going in, and stepped out.

Holding the sides of her dress's skirt so they wouldn't rustle as she followed the unsuspecting soul, giving away her curiosity, she tiptoed down the street. Past the stationery shop, whose flower boxes bobbed with snowdrops, past the supermarket, past the butcher's. Where on earth were they going? They were quickly running out of shops and the last place on the small strip of street was The Bullion.

Ice ran through her veins. Surely not? Tony hadn't started opening early, had he? Taken her coffee business away from her? They had a deal. He wouldn't serve coffee until after she'd closed.

But she had closed.

Not forever, though. At least, she hadn't had solid plans to close forever. Or maybe she had, but she'd not announced them or left town. The least he could do was wait until she'd packed up and gone.

Surely enough, her prey made a beeline for the old pub. Mel stopped short, her fists clenched at her side, her nails dug into the palms of her hand. Something was different about the place. It looked brighter. More welcoming. The big door, always closed, was propped open with an old wine barrel. Even from ten metres away she could see the curtains were pulled back and the dingy old windows gleamed clean. Had Tony not made enough money to save himself from having The Bullion taken away and sold to the highest bidder? If that were the case, she could forgive him for treading on her turf. If not? Well, his ears weren't only good for nibbling on; she was pretty sure they were the perfect size for pulling him outside and giving him a public dressing-down.

Plan made, mind made up, she strode to the front door and burst through to see what looked like half the town sitting down and chatting gaily, their hands wrapped around mugs and cups, plates of food in various stages of being eaten in front of them.

Okay, so Tony had sold up. Given up. Not only on her, but on his first love. That was the only explanation. Mel tried to ignore the sadness blooming in her chest. Her chance of discovering real love had gone. Not that there'd been much of a chance, not after the way she'd treated Tony. But she had dared to hope he could forgive her, give her a second chance, this time at a proper relationship.

Whoever had bought the pub had some money to splash around, though. Mel took in the cream, brocade curtains lining the windows, pulled back with light-olive green-silk sashes, the same colour as the freshly painted walls. The leaners were still there, but instead of being rickety-old and formica-topped, they'd been converted to more of the wine barrels she'd seen outside. Surrounding them were stools, covered in a yellow fabric, not dissimilar to the sun- shine yellow she'd painted her lounge. That same fabric was on the dining chairs in the newly created café area, where so many of the townsfolk were enjoying breakfast, each wooden table topped with a white tablecloth and a vintage vase filled with fresh flowers. The new owners may have stolen her business, but at least they had taste.

'Take a seat, I'll be with you in a minute.'

Mel's head snapped to the bar area where the order had come from. Heat bloomed in her cheeks, hope in her heart. Tony was still here. He hadn't gone, after all. But he had encroached on her territory, and he needed to know that was not cool.

'Ma'am?' Tony indicated to the empty table near the window, his face still with concentration as he gazed into the milk jug. 'That's a great seat. The sun's coming in, it'll keep you warm.'

It dawned on Mel that he didn't realise who she was. Mel in clacky little heels and a ladylike dress? He'd never expect that. Well, he'd realise it was her soon enough.

'I shall do no such thing. I don't eat at establishments that steal my business despite clear rules being set about when we can operate around each other. We had a deal.'

Tony's head snapped up and his eyes widened as he took in her dress, her shoes. Her hair. Mel's hand unconsciously went to the newly lightened locks.

'You're blonde?' Tony stepped out from behind the bar and cautiously walked towards her. Did he think he was dreaming? Did he not trust his eyes?

'I am.' Mel nodded, unsure of what to do or what to say next. She'd never been shy in front of Tony before, not even after their first night of lovemaking. But the way he was looking at her right now? Why wasn't there a rock she could hide under? Perhaps the wine barrels were hollow? She could scurry into one of those…

'You know, I thought your mother might have adopted you. You were so different from…'

'I know. I mean, I am different from her, in temperament. But we do look quite similar, when I allow myself to.'

'And am I dreaming?' Tony rubbed his eyes, then dropped his hand to his side, a grin on his face. 'Are you wearing a dress? A pretty one?'

Mel spun round. 'You like? I have a wardrobe full of them.'

'I more than like.' He took a step towards her. His hand reached for hers.

'Oh no you don't, buddy.' Mel ducked out of reach. Did he think she was going to let him off the hook just because he smiled that drop-dead-gorgeous smile of his? 'We have a whole bunch to talk about. What is this?' She waved to the dining area. 'I'll be broke within a week. I can't believe you'd steal my business away from me. Is this your way of getting back at me?'

Tony shrugged, a sparkle appearing in his eye. 'Well, you shut up shop. People were hungry. I figured something had to be done, and since there was an opening in the market...'

'You could've called me. Or texted me. Or come round to see me and we could've talked about it...'

'Well, I got the impression from our last conversation that you didn't want anything to do with me. Or anyone for that matter. So I wasn't going to rest on my laurels while you hid away and rued the biggest mistake you've ever made.'

Mel's hands flew to her hips. '"Biggest mistake I've ever made"?'

Tony dipped his head towards her. 'Well I figured you'd eventually realise that I was the man for you.' His voice was low, intimate, self-assured. 'That you and I were meant to be together and not just in some crazy, fake-fiancé, business-saving relationship.'

Mel's hands tightened on her hips. What was he saying? That he still wanted to be with her? After everything? But it made no sense... 'You know, if you want to be with someone, if you want to woo them, you generally don't destroy their business.'

'Like I said, I saw an opening in the market and thought, why not?' Tony grinned, sending Mel's stomach into knots of suspicion. And desire. Why did he have to be so damn handsome? So insanely irresistible? 'I was also thinking about doing lunches...'

'You weren't!?' Mel's mouth formed a perfect 'o' of horror. Was he trying to drive her away?

'And, of course, delicious food in the evenings.'

'But you've only just started learning to cook. How do you plan on making all this happen?' Mel took in the newly refurbished space. 'And how'd you make all *this* happen?'

Tony took her hand in his, warm, strong, capable. Part of her screamed 'run'. Yelled at her for not pushing away the man who was working to destroy what security she'd created. But another part of her refused to budge, told her to wait, to see what he had to say for himself. For once, she let that small, trusting part she'd buried away win.

'Well, I got to thinking about what you have to do to nurture the things you love. You have to put time in, effort, think about what would make them happy. Things I haven't done with The Bullion, despite loving it as much as I do. I also realised you had to let someone help you out. Dad didn't build this pub all on his own, he had Mum there every step of the way, encouraging him, supporting him, helping him out in the kitchen, all while raising us kids until she was taken from us.'

A lump formed in Mel's throat. She'd felt angry at having a mother who was erratic, yet Tony had barely had one at all.

'Don't be sad for me, Mel. I'm a big boy. I've had time to grieve, for both of them, but it's time for The Bullion transformed from a memorial into the living, breathing heart of the community again.'

Mel squeezed Tony's hand and took a small step towards him. He looked so sad, so stricken, yet she could feel determination radiating from him, a sense of renewed energy.

'The thing is, Mel. I've met someone.'

What? He'd met someone? Yet he was looking at her like he adored her? What kind of player was this guy? She tried to shake her hand out of his, but he gripped it more firmly.

'I met a woman who is without a doubt the sexiest thing I've ever seen. Feisty, too.'

'I don't want to hear about you and your floozies.' Mel spat the words out and focused on the gleaming lights in the fridges behind the bar. Trying to stop the hope she'd held inside her heart from flowing down her cheeks.

'I wouldn't call this woman a floozy. I'd call her beautiful. She was a tiny wee thing, with chin-length black hair with crazy pink stripes, and she always wore black. Something I never thought I'd find desirable and yet I never thought I'd want anyone more… until now.'

***

Mel's eyes dawned with understanding. The flinty hardness was replaced with a warmth that turned her chocolate-brown eyes a stunning amber.

'This woman changed me, Mel. She showed me that change wasn't a bad thing, that success meant being brave and doing things differently. She doesn't know it, but she gave me the courage to write a business plan, to put on a suit and visit the bank manager in the next town over. I don't know what the guy was thinking, but he gave me a loan that'd have some of the farmers round here choking on their wellingtons, and then he told me to go ahead and make my dreams come true.'

'And just what are those dreams?' Mel's voice was choked with emotion. He could feel her hand quivering in his. He ached to pull her towards him, to feel her perfect curves meld with his body, but he held off. She needed to understand how serious he was about her. She needed to know she was his forever.

'To turn The Bullion into a destination for locals, those living in the closest towns, and for those from further afield. A boutique hotel serving only the best and freshest food. I've taken steps to set up a proper craft brewery and I'm in talks with a few places that might stock the beer once all the necessary paperwork is through.'

'You've been busy…'

'I've been inspired.' He wrapped his arm around her waist and pulled her to him.

'Inspired by the girl with the black-and-pink hair?' Mel's hand touched her now-fair hair.

'That's the one. But you see, I'm a fickle man. You've told me as much a million times. And just now a woman walked in wearing a smoking-hot dress and this beautiful blonde hair and I can't say I'm not interested. In fact, I'm very interested.'

'So you'd dump the other girl for this one? Just like that?'

'The other girl didn't want me. I tried my best to make her see that we'd be perfect together, forever, too… I was quite heartbroken. But it spurred me on to do all this… for her.'

'For her?' Mel angled her head, her eyebrows arrowed together in confusion. 'Why would you do all this for a woman who didn't want you?'

'Because I thought we had a future together. Thought maybe we could run this place together…' Tony took a deep breath and nodded to the kitchen door. His heart hammered in his chest. If things were going to go the way he wanted, the way he'd planned, he was about to find out. Or to have his dreams dashed.

Mel followed his gaze to the sign he'd carefully nailed above the kitchen door. A sign he'd spent hours carving, working through the night, ignoring the blisters and the cuts and the finger cramps to get it done in time for today, his grand reopening.

He looked down at Mel and watched for her reaction. Prayed it would be the one he was hoping for.

Her eyes narrowed. Widened. Lips parted as she mouthed the words on the sign.

'Mel's.'

Tony mashed his lips together. Did she understand what that sign meant? Would she realise the magnitude of it?

'So…' Her pixie face turned to face him. 'You want me to close my café and go into business with you? I don't think so, buddy. I've worked long and hard to build Mel's. I'm not closing it for anyone.'

Tony inwardly groaned. Had she misread his intentions that badly?

A smile tugged at the corner of Mel's lips. Was she teasing him? Or was she just happy? Tony squirmed as uncertainty took hold. Had this been a mistake? Was he in danger of losing Mel? He needed her to make everything work. More importantly, he simply needed her.

'Well, I mean… I was hoping you'd advise me on the menus like we originally talked about.' Tony ran his hand through his hair. Was she getting this at all? 'And, um, maybe you could also stay upstairs…'

'You want me to move out of my apartment and up into one of those gloomy rooms? With the back-breaking mattresses? Just to be your advisor? Are you kidding me?' Her arms left his waist as she took a step backwards and pointed at him. 'I am used to a certain level of comfort, Tony McArthur. I may have given it up in order to be your fake fiancée for one hot minute, but I am not doing that again.'

'What if I had a new mattress installed? Because I did budget for that. But there's one catch.'

'And what would that be?'

Tony took hold of her slim hips and brought her close, so close he could feel her heart thumping against his chest. 'If I'm to get a new mattress in, then you'll have to sleep with me, in my room. As my real fiancée.'

'As your? What?' Mel's smile bloomed, her face lighting up from ear to ear.

'You heard me. I want you, Mel. Not just as my business partner, but as my life partner.' Tony shuddered. 'I hate that word.'

Mel giggled. 'Yeah, me too.'

He dropped a quick kiss on her lips. 'I want to share my life with you, Mel. With you by my side I feel like a man who can conquer anything. So will you say yes?'

'To your deal? Or to moving in with you?'

'To marrying me.' Tony bent down on one knee and tried to ignore the hushed whispers of excitement coming from the tables surrounding them. 'Melanie Sullivan, I love you with all my heart. You've changed me, given me real purpose, shown me how to be a better man. I can't live another day without you... and your food knowledge.' He grinned as Mel rolled her eyes while titters of laughter spread around the room. 'Melanie, will you do me the honour of moving in with me, of being my fiancée, the love of my life, and eventually my wife?' He pulled a black velvet box from his jeans pocket and opened it, revealing a pink sapphire, surrounded by diamonds in a vintage-style, white-gold setting. The sapphire was the same shade Mel's hair had been. He swallowed nervously. Would she like it even though her hair had changed? He'd dithered for an hour at the jeweller's over what to buy until the poor saleswoman had taken five rings, put them on her fingers, then had him remove them one by one until he was left with the ring he felt most represented Mel. Unique, beautiful, classic with a twist. 'Say yes, Mel. I promise you won't ever regret it.'

Tension was thick in the air as the diners waited for

an answer. Forks paused in mid-air, coffee going cold in their cups.

Mel took in the man down on bended knee before her. His arm raised, and holding a dainty velvet box containing the most beautiful piece of jewellery she'd ever seen in her life. A faint sheen appeared at his temples, the corner of his eye twitched, a slight frown appeared, crinkling his handsome brow.

Was this really happening? To her? After all these years of trying to create a life of security, of working to make a place truly her home, was it really being offered up to her on a plate? Or in the form of a ring?

'Mel?' Tony's word was a whisper. 'The floor's not carpeted any more and, well, my knee's not as young as it used to be...'

Mel took his hand in hers and lifted him up. 'I'll marry you on one condition.'

Tony's brow furrowed even more deeply. 'What's that?'

'You have to promise to sell that beast of a machine you bought and get your coffee orders from me, and any desserts you serve will come from me, too.' She held out her left hand, fingers spread and raised an eyebrow in expectation. 'Is this arrangement acceptable to you?'

She watched as fumbling fingers removed the ring and slid it onto her ring finger. 'Absolutely, especially because my coffee's even worse than you said it would be.'

The pub erupted in cheers of joy and laughter, coffee

cups clanked as their engagement was toasted, tables thumped in approval.

'I guess that means we have an arrangement,' Tony said, wrapping his arms around her waist and pulling her towards him. His lips lowered to hers and they kissed, tender, slow, with no urgency, the kiss of two people who had a lifetime of kisses to look forward to.

After a time, Tony's lips left hers and he smiled, soft and sweet. 'Welcome home, Mel.'

ACKNOWLEDGEMENTS

To my husband. From the day I came home and told you I was going to write romance novels you never once doubted me. Thank you for sitting opposite me every morning at our local café while I banged out words and drank my flat white. Thank you for giving me the opportunity to chase my dreams. Thank you for being you.

To Louisa George. I thought I'd struck gold when you agreed to be my mentor. Gold? More like diamonds. Thank you for pushing and supporting me. As a mentor and a friend, you're a gem.

To Susie Frame. Thank you for your thoughtful advice, support and friendship. Oh, and the comma policing. Best critique partner, ever.

To Chris and Peter Hailes, Laura Hancox, Natalie Gillespie and Wendi Lane for putting up with my endless questions and never failing to come through with an answer.

To my amazing editor, Victoria Oundjian. Thank you for giving my characters a chance to see the light of day. Thank you for making my dream come true.

Turn the page for an exclusive extract
from *The Little Unicorn Gift Shop*...

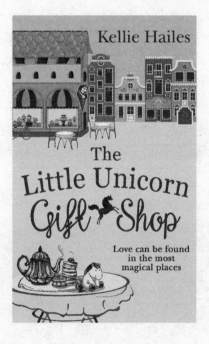

CHAPTER ONE

An ear-piercing trilling ripped Ben from the soundest sleep he'd had in weeks. His hand blindly scrambled round his bedside table, searching for his phone. Who could be calling at this time of night? He'd collapsed into bed just after midnight, so he knew it had to be late. He peeled open one eye. It was nowhere-near-dawn kind of late if the pitch-blackness in his room was anything to go by. Finding the phone, he squinted against the glare of the screen to see who would be so rude as to ring at such an ungodly hour.

His heart, already thumping from the shock of being yanked out of his sleep, ratcheted up to a worrying state.

Poppy.

Apprehension settled heavy in his stomach. If she was calling at this time of night it couldn't be for any good reason.

He peered at the screen. Not a phone call, a video call. Well, that ruled out her being in prison, at least. He was pretty sure they still only allowed voice calls.

He glanced at the time. Just gone three. Which made

it the afternoon, maybe, if she was still in New Zealand. Though knowing Poppy, she could have tired of the place and moved on to South America, where no doubt she'd be in a jungle hugging a tree in protest of it and its foliage-filled friends being cut down.

He swiped across and watched the internet decide whether it was going to connect him to her or not. A creased forehead and impatient stare gave him his answer.

'Ben? You there? Ben? Can you hear me?'

Ben clicked the sound down and reminded himself to mute his phone before he went to sleep from now on. 'I hear you, Poppy.' He stifled a yawn. 'Where are you? Are you okay? Are you in trouble? Do you need bail money?'

'Of course I'm okay.' Poppy rolled her eyes. 'I'm not a teenager, Ben. You don't have to keep me from getting into trouble anymore. Not that you could've if you wanted to. And bail money? Really? I've never been in that kind of trouble. God, dramatic much?'

'Fair enough. Sorry, Pops, but when I get a call in the middle of the night I fear the worst.' Ben folded his pillow in half and elbowed his way into a half-sitting position.

'Fine. Whatever. And turn on your light. It's weird talking to the black hole of Ben.'

'Sorry. Forgot you couldn't see me.' Ben switched the phone to his other hand, then leaned over and flicked on the bedside lamp. Its golden glow illuminated the small space around him.

'Geez, Ben, what've you been doing?' Poppy's hand covered her eyes, her fingers splitting apart to peek through at him. 'Do you even work these days? Or do you spend all your waking hours at the gym?'

'Huh?' Ben peered at the square on the phone to see what Poppy was seeing. 'Oh, God, sorry, Pops.' He pulled the sheet up to his armpits. 'There, all decent.'

Poppy's hand fell down, a wide grin lifting her cheekbones high as strands of her black hair blew in front of her face. 'Ugh, blimmin' wind. It's so cold I'm amazed my lips haven't frozen together. I'll be glad to come home to a bit of warmth.'

Ben straightened up in bed. Had he heard what he thought he'd heard? 'Come home? What are you on about?'

'Well, I've been travelling for over a decade now. It's time I returned. I mean, look at this place. It's freezing. My plane ticket's all booked.' She switched the phone's camera around and moved it slowly, showing him a snow-covered mountain range that sloped down to a tumultuous grey-green sea, its waves crashing onto a beach smothered in time-smoothed stones.

'It's beautiful,' Ben observed. 'And it gets freezing here too, remember?'

The camera switched back to Poppy. 'Yeah, but here is not home, and it's time.'

'And why are you telling me this, Poppy?' Ben yawned,

not bothering to hide his tiredness. He had a busy day at the office ahead of him tying up loose ends, and he had to make sure his finances were in order for when he viewed the shop he hoped to lease in three days' time. 'More importantly, can you make it quick? It's beyond the middle of the night and I've got to get some sleep if I'm going to function like a human being tomorrow.'

'Fine, fine, Mr Busy Pants.' Poppy grinned. 'I just need you to do me a favour and pick me up from Heathrow. I'll send you through the details.' She flapped a hand in his direction. 'Now go back to sleep. Get some rest. I'll see you soon.' She blew a kiss and wiggled her fingers in goodbye, before signing off, leaving Ben staring at a Poppy-less screen.

Poppy Taylor was coming home.

An email alert popped up on his screen. He opened it and scanned the contents.

Not only was Poppy Taylor coming home, she was having him pick her up on the day he was meeting with his potential landlord. He worked out the time it would take to drive from Heathrow to Muswell Hill. He could do it. Just assuming traffic wasn't awful.

You could just say no…

He untucked his pillow and settled back into bed. As if no was an option. No was never an option where Poppy was concerned. Even after all these years.

CHAPTER TWO

'Excuse me.' Poppy dodged and ducked her way through the throng of people squealing, hugging and, sometimes, crying into each other's arms as family, friends and lovers arrived from their various destinations. Every few seconds she went on tiptoe to search the crowd waiting at arrivals for a familiar face. Not just a familiar face, a friendly one. 'Where is he?' she wondered aloud, as she hefted her bulging backpack a little higher to stop the waist belt further cutting into her hips.

'Poppy?'

She spun round and found herself gazing into warm brown eyes. The very same pair that had greeted her when she'd poked her head through the hedge that had bordered their properties when they were four years old.

'Ben.' She wrapped her arms around him and pulled him into a hug. The muscles she'd briefly viewed during their video call were no figment of her imagination. Ben was *toned*. 'Now tell me…' She pulled back and squeezed his biceps. 'Where did these come from?'

Ben shrugged, a faint glow rising on his cheeks. 'I swim at the gym every morning. Then do weights if I feel like it.'

'All that on top of being a fancy pants lawyer?' Poppy threaded her arm through Ben's and let him lead her through the crowds. 'Do you ever sleep?'

'I do. When I'm not being woken in the middle of the night.' He nudged her with his elbow. 'Now can we up the pace? I've got a business meeting I have to get to.'

'All work and no play makes Ben a—'

'Makes Ben a late boy. And I can't be. I'm opening a business. Well, I'm planning to. But I need to secure the premises first, and I think I've found the perfect spot.'

Poppy quickened her step as Ben pulled her through the busy airport, ducking out of the way of the dawdling travellers. 'Business? What kind of business? And how do you plan on running a business when you've a day job and apparently one hot bod to maintain?'

Ben's cheeks lost their blush as he propelled her to the carpark and towards a sleek, black Audi. 'This is me.' He opened the door for her, then strode to his side of the car and got in. 'And I won't be doing both jobs. I'm leaving law.'

'You say that like it's the end of the world.' Poppy ran her hands over the seat's buttery leather. Ben was leaving a job that had bought him *this* to set up a shop? And it sounded as though the thought of it was making him sick. Or perhaps it was the risk? Taking risks wasn't

Ben's way. He'd always been the solid, dependable one. The one who made his parents proud... Ah. The green tinge to his skin suddenly made sense. Ben's father was a lawyer. Ben had done as expected and followed his father into law. Leaving it couldn't have been easy on Ben. And she'd have bet all of the worldly goods she owned, all that were tucked into the backpack Ben had placed into the boot of the car, that his father wouldn't be making his defection easy on him.

'Buckled up?' Ben started the engine and focused on the backup mirror's camera as he reversed out of the park.

Poppy relaxed into the seat and took a moment to inspect her old friend. Twelve years had changed him, and yet he was the same. Fine lines framing the outer corners of his eyes crinkled as he focused on the road. Time had seen the soft curves of his jawline and cheeks evaporate into sharp lengths. Yet, as always, his chin and cheeks were bare of stubble. Still, there was no denying Ben's boyish good looks were there, albeit more...manly. Stronger. Defined. The kind that probably had women's knees going a little – or a lot – wobbly when he walked past. Poppy patted her knees. Solid as two knobbly rocks. Ben may have been good to look at – better than good – but he was the serious, settling down type. And she wasn't. Which made her interest in Ben strictly platonic.

'Could you stop staring?' The corners of his lips lifted up into a smile. 'I feel like a bug under a microscope.'

Ben's eyes flicked in her direction, then refocused on the road. Yep, between that smile and those eyes, and the rest of the Ben-shaped package, Poppy suspected Ben had more than his share of admirers.

'Sorry, Ben the Bug, can't help it. It's been *ages*.' Poppy stretched her legs, and circled her neck backwards then forwards to release the tension of being cooped up in a metal bird for so many hours. 'You don't do social media so I can't stalk photos of you, and you haven't picked up a video call from me in longer than I can remember, so I feel like I'm seeing you for the first time in *forever*.'

'I didn't pick up your calls because you call during work hours.'

'I figured that, eventually. That's why I called in the middle of the night. I knew you'd have to answer.' Poppy unzipped her carry-on bag, found a tube of lip balm and applied it, smacking her lips together in satisfaction. She may have had years away from Ben, with minimal contact, but that didn't mean she didn't know him.

'I could have had my phone turned off. Or on silent.'

Poppy grinned at his churlish tone. 'Not the Ben I know. He's far too responsible. If your parents needed you, or if work was to have some kind of emergency, I knew you'd need to be on hand to deal with it.'

'Wow, you make me sound boring... and in need of a life.' A frown sent lines sprawling across Ben's forehead.

'Don't get all upset about it, Ben. I'm not saying you're

boring, or in need of a life. I just knew you'd answer, that's all.' Poppy crossed her arms over her chest and tucked her hands into her armpits. Since when had Ben become so touchy?

'No, it's not you. It's the time. It's later than I thought. And this driver in front of me is going at a snail's pace.' The car surged forward as Ben stepped on the accelerator and manoeuvred into the next lane.

Poppy released her hands and gripped onto the edges of the seat. 'Steady on, Ben. No need to speed.'

'I'm not.' He flapped his hand at the speedometer. 'There's no way I'm going to get pulled over and make myself even later.' He ran his hand through his short, sandy brown hair. The same cut he'd always had. Shorter on the sides, with a little length up top. 'No, it'll be fine. It has to be.'

'Do you want me to call the landlord for you? Explain you'll be late?' Poppy held out her hand. 'My phone's dead. Give me yours.'

'No, not a good idea. That'll make me look like I'm unreliable. He might think I'll be late with payments. I was hoping to have time to pop home and grab a fresh shirt, but I'll just have to make do with the one I keep spare in the back. It's not the exact right shade to go with the tie or jacket, but it'll do. It'll have to.'

Poppy bit a laugh back, sensing that giggling at Ben's super-serious suit dilemma when he was this stressed would only inflame the situation.

'And you'll have to wait in the car before I drop you… wait, where am I dropping you?' Ben's eyebrow cocked as he glanced at her. 'You never said. Are you staying at your mum's house?'

Poppy's stomach shrivelled. She took a deep breath as the unappetising meal of frittata and fruit salad they'd been served on the plane threatened to deboard. Stay with her mother? Not if she could help it. The plan was to keep her distance as long as possible. Why invite pain back into her life when she'd spent twelve years trying to keep it out? She waved the suggestion away. 'No, not Mum's. I've found a flat in Muswell Hill. And waiting is fine. I've nowhere to be. I'll just work on my plans while you have your meeting.'

'Plans? Since when has Poppy Taylor planned anything? You didn't even plan leaving to head off overseas. You just took off.'

There was no missing the bitter edge to Ben's words, but no way was Poppy going to explain why she left. Not to Ben of all people. The events that had led to her leaving were best left well alone.

'I'm not eighteen anymore, Ben. Believe it or not, I've become rather good at planning and organising. You have to when you're travelling. When you move around a lot. The thing is, you're not the only one who's planning on starting a business. I've one in mind, too. A gift shop, featuring all things unicorn. And I think Muswell Hill may well be the perfect place to set up shop.'

Ben's lips quirked, then mashed together, then quirked up again.

'What? You think I'm not serious? You don't think I can?' Poppy re-folded her arms, more to stop herself from punching Ben in the arm than to shield herself from his amused disbelief.

Ben's chest rose and fell, his lips straightened out. 'It's not that I don't think you can, I just didn't expect you to say that. I mean, a business is a lot of work. You can't just flit in and out. You have to think ahead. You have to be serious. And, well, just how serious is a unicorn gift shop?'

'It's very serious. You wouldn't know. You've spent your working life with your head in textbooks and papers and whatnot. Your lack of online presence alone tells me you've no idea about the explosion of unicorn everything. People love them. Not just kids either. Teens. People in their twenties. Thirties. *Everyone*. There are webpages dedicated to them. My social media feeds are dotted with random snaps of them. They're huge. Which means my unicorn gift shop is going to draw crowds from all around, you'll see.' Poppy gave a definitive nod. Ben's reaction only added fuel to her plans. He thought she was the same old flighty, fun Poppy? Well, he was going to find out otherwise. 'Anyway, you never told me what business you were planning to open?' Poppy gazed out at the window, her heart picking up pace as she took in the streets whizzing past. As familiar to her as the back of her hand, these were streets she'd roamed day and night, her mother giving her more freedom than any child should ever have. Freedom, when what she'd really wanted was love. To feel loved. To feel wanted. The only person who'd made her feel that way sat next to her. But that was a long time ago. Things had changed. *She* had changed.

'A gourmet tea shop.' Ben expertly parallel parked outside a row of houses around the corner from the shops. 'High-end teas sourced from around the globe. Delicious cakes. Slices. Biscuits.'

'And who'll be making these cakes and slices? You?' Poppy released her seatbelt and got out of the car. She lifted her arms in a long stretch, breathed in the sun-warmed air, and allowed herself a small smile as she took in the terraced homes, many fronted by perfectly clipped hedges perched atop matching brick fences. So different to the wooden one-storeyed Sixties-style bungalows and Eighties-built styleless square boxes that had lined the street she'd lived on last.

The slam of the car door brought her attention back to Ben, who was expertly knotting his tie.

'Yes, me.' He scooped up a suit jacket and shrugged it on, then buttoned it up. 'I'll be doing the baking.'

'Really?' Poppy released the stretch, then leaned against the car. 'I know you were the king of Home Economics at school but baking at school is one thing – baking for business is another.'

'And you'd know this how?' Ben locked his car and started up the street.

'Am I coming with you?' Poppy trailed after him. 'I thought I was to stay with the car.'

'You can come for the walk if you want. I'd have thought you'd be tired of being stuck inside. Or you can stay here. Do what you want. I don't care.'

He could say he didn't care, but the squaring of his shoulders and the frostiness in his voice told her otherwise. *Stupid Poppy.* She'd just pooh-poohed his business idea. Pooh-poohed him. It was one thing to listen to her horrid inner critic that always tried to make her second-guess her abilities, her worth, but she had no right to project that inner critic onto Ben. Not when she knew how determined and disciplined Ben could be. He could have taken night classes. Watched online tutorials. Done any number of things to learn how to bake for the masses, and she wouldn't know. Their steady stream of communication when she'd first left had turned into a trickle over the years as Ben had become busier. His emails shorter. To the point. And, eventually, she'd got the point, Ben didn't have time for her. Yet she'd still emailed on occasion, whenever she moved, just so someone at home knew where she was in case anything went wrong.

Poppy jogged a few steps to catch up with Ben. 'Sorry, I didn't mean to offend you. I'm an idiot. I should know better. Whenever you put your mind to something you make it work. More than that, you succeed. You always have. I bet you could enter a baking competition on the telly and win. Easily.'

'I bet I could too. And it's not like I stopped baking once I left school. It's been my stress relief for as long as I can remember. It also made me very popular at work when I brought in the previous night's goods.' Ben turned onto a bustling side street, dotted with shops that hadn't been there when she left. A generic chain-store coffee shop, a designer clothing store, a store selling cutesy baby gear. She spotted the charity store where she'd got most of her wardrobe from as a youngster. Got? More like stolen. Hunching in the doorway in the middle of the night, rifling through bags left at the door, praying she wouldn't be caught, not wanting to admit to anyone that her mother was too busy with her art and friends and gregarious lifestyle to be bothered to think her daughter might need clothes. To be bothered to think, or care, about her daughter at all.

Give big anonymous donation to store. Poppy added the thought to the top of her mental 'to-do' list.

Next to the charity store stood an empty shop, a 'for lease' sign hanging in its window. Was the sign a sign? Was that the shop she could set up her business in? Lightness infused her heart, dispersing the dread she hadn't realised had been sitting dark and heavy. She'd take note of the number and call the shop's owner once she was settled in her new place.

Ben crossed the street then stopped in front of the shop. *Her* shop. No, surely not. He wasn't stealing her shop from underneath her, was he? Not that he knew it was her shop, but it had to be. She felt it deep down. The same way she'd known deep down that it was time to come home.

'How do I look?' He straightened his shoulders, ran his hand over his perfect-as-always hair and flashed her a winning smile.

'Perfect. Is the shop around the corner? On the main road?'

'No. It's this one, right here.' He angled his head towards the space. 'It suits my budget, and the street's busy, and close enough to the main street that people won't be put off making a small detour to visit.'

'You've thought it all out.' Of course he had. That's what Ben did. His life had been mapped out since he was young. He didn't do anything without careful thought. The opposite of herself. She'd figured she'd come home, find a flat, nab herself a space, place an order for a bunch of cute unicorn products and watch the customers and money roll in. She'd not even thought about budgets, other than to have enough money in the bank to start the business.

The squeak of the front door snapped her out of her darkening mood. 'Mr Evans? You're on time. Excellent. I like that. You didn't mention anything about bringing someone? No matter though. There's not much to see, just the main space, the kitchen behind, and there's a small office. But it's always good to have a second opinion. Come in. Come in. Lovely to meet you, dear, I'm Monty Gilbert. Call me Monty.'

'Actually, she was going to stay out—' Ben went to correct the bespectacled gentleman who'd greeted him, but stopped as he was hustled inside.

Poppy gave him a 'what can you do' shrug, trailed inside and then stepped to the right, giving Ben some space to chat to the landlord and giving herself a moment to view the shop that would have been hers if Ben hadn't seen it first.

It was beautiful. Perfect. Polished wooden floors gleamed under subtle downlights. One end of the shop was lined in redbrick, the other plastered and painted a barely-there cream. She could imagine white-painted shelves pushed up against it, filled with unicorn stationery – holographic pens, unicorn stickers, writing sets. Mugs from bombastic and brilliant to sweet and subtle. Stuffed unicorn toys could take pride of place in the corner, and a range of unicorn-printed clothing could hang from a rack by the far wall.

She glanced over at Ben and saw his eyes brighten as he took in the brick wall. She knew what he was seeing. She could see it too. Wooden shelving stained the colour of long-steeped black tea would be perfect against that red and would look marvellous holding tea-sets and tins of tea. And the ornate timber counter could easily be stained the same colour and would provide a striking centrepiece for the shop. It was the perfect space for his venture.

'I must apologise, I was a little misleading in my advertisement.' Monty shoved his hands in the pockets of his brown corduroy and rocked back and forth on his feet. 'You see my son told me I was asking too little rent for this space. I haven't had to rent it out in years, you see. The only reason I'm renting it now is because the previous tenant passed, may she rest in peace, and I thought a little hike in the lease was fine. Turns out I was going to be doing myself no favours...'

'Oh.' Ben's face stilled. His eyes narrowed. Was that panic flashing through them? Or had Poppy imagined it? 'What kind of rent are you looking for?'

Monty paused, then uttered a number.

The colour drained from Ben's face. 'That's twice what you were asking in the advertisement.'

'I know, and I'm sorry if I've wasted your time.' Monty looked up as the door opened and two gangly teens walked in. A boy and a girl, both the same height, with hair the identical shade of auburn.

Fraternal twins, Poppy guessed.

'Sophie, Joseph. Didn't I tell you to wait outside if you saw I was with people?' Monty folded his arms and fixed the twins with an irritated stare.

'Sorry, Grandad. Forgot.' The girl, Sophie, shrugged, then held up her hand and began inspecting her nails.

Monty's chest rose and fell as a huff of irritation filled the room. 'I'm so sorry for the intrusion, Mr Evans. Would you mind giving me a minute while I sort these two out, then send them on their way?' His palms flipped up in a silent apology, before turning his attention to the twins. 'So, how did the job search go?' Monty's pitch heightened with hope.

'Nowhere.' Sophie leaned against the counter, her petite nose wrinkling. 'The job search went nowhere, right, Joe?'

Her brother nodded, his eyes fixed on the floorboards. 'Nobody wants us.'

'And we tried, Grandad, we really did.' Sophie pulled out her phone and buried her nose in it.

Poppy grinned. Sure they'd tried. That explained the splodge of what looked like chocolate ice cream on Joseph's shirt. And the leaf attached to the bottom of Sophie's shoe. Grabbing ice cream and going for a walk through Queen's Wood was hardly what she'd call a job search.

'Well, you'll have to try again tomorrow.' Monty shook his head. 'I can't have you two underfoot all holidays. And I promised your parents we'd keep you busy, keep you out of mischief, until you decided what you wanted to do with your lives.'

An idea swirled in the back of Poppy's mind. She may

have found a way to launch both businesses, while getting onside with the landlord, who – if the look of despair on his face was anything to go by – had two charges on his hands that were going to drive him crazy if they weren't kept busy.

'How much did you say the rent was again?' She made her way to stand beside Ben, hoping he'd go along with her idea. Provide a united front.

Monty repeated the price.

'Would you consider shaving ten per cent off that, in exchange for hiring these two?' She nodded at Sophie and Joe, whose mouths formed identical o's, their aquamarine eyes widening in horror. Poppy suppressed a smile. 'Because we're going to need some help, Ben and I, if we're going to open our shops in this space in a couple of weeks' time.'

'Our shops?' Ben shot Poppy a quizzical look.

'Sparkle & Steep. That's the name we agreed on, right?' She raised her eyebrows, praying that Ben wouldn't work against her.

'Sparkle & Steep. Yes, that's right.' Ben nodded, his face free from emotion.

A bit shell-shocked, Poppy guessed. 'You see, Monty, we are going to open a gourmet tea shop, and London's most fabulous unicorn gift shop.' She turned to her new employees. 'Now, Sophie, Joe, I may as well be upfront about this. We can't afford to pay much, I'm sorry, but being new and all there's just not the money there for more than the living wage.'

'That's fine,' Monty interrupted. 'These two need work, and you're offering it. It'll keep them out of my hair, and keep them out of trouble. I've got the papers all drawn up out back. Take a look at them, and if all is in order, the shop's yours. But the sooner you decide the better, I've another interested party keen to take a look. They should be here any minute, actually.' Not waiting for an answer Monty turned and made his way through the door to the back room, leaving the two teens to huddle up in a murmur of mutters.

Ben pulled Poppy to the furthest corner. 'What are you doing?' he hissed. 'Opening a store with me? That wasn't the plan. And why'd you go and throw the twins into the deal? They clearly don't want to work.'

'First of all, you had your budget and this was out of it. I, too, have a budget.' Poppy crossed her fingers behind her back. 'And our budgets combined will make this work. Also, you'll need help. And I'll need help. And it's clear to me that Monty is being driven round the bend by those two being under his feet. It all makes sense. I'd go so far as to say it's meant to be.' Poppy flashed Ben a thumbs up, along with an encouraging nod.

Monty returned in a rustle of paper and a hustle of feet. 'Here you go. Here are the papers. Look over them. It's all above board, but I want you to be happy.'

Poppy thrust her hand in Monty's direction, and ignored Ben's choke-cough. 'No need for that. I trust you. We trust you. Consider us your new tenants.'

CHAPTER THREE

Ben ran his eyes over the documents before him. Poppy may have been willing to sign away her life without checking things out first, but there was no way he was about to. Still, they looked fine to his professional eye. Everything was in order as Monty had said. But what was not in order, in fact what was highly *out* of order, was Poppy springing this on him without even considering his thoughts, his feelings.

Sharing a space with her? Not just a space, but a business space? This wasn't like sharing a fake pet rock as they had when they were young and neither set of parents had allowed them to own a puppy or kitten. This was their lives. Their livelihoods. And if the fate of their pet rock was anything to go by, going into business with Poppy was not a good idea. She'd lost the darn thing between school and home three days into their deal to share it.

'Didn't see that coming, did ya?' The girl – Sophie – nudged him with her elbow. 'I've never seen someone look so green in my life. Do you need a bucket?'

'Sophie, don't be rude. That's our boss you're talking to.' Her brother pulled Sophie away and gave Ben some breathing space.

Breathing space? He'd need more than the air in the shop to breathe after everything Poppy had just flung at him. He'd need a small country's worth of air. Speaking of Poppy, where had she gone? 'Poppy?'

'I'm out the back. With you in a sec.'

The light tip-tap of excitable feet greeted him, followed by Poppy, her green eyes sparkling with excitement.

'This place is perfect. The kitchen's great. You'll love it. The office is a little small, but I'm sure we can take turns in there to have our cups of tea when we're on break, or eat our lunch, or whatever. Or we could squeeze in together if you don't mind getting cuddly with me. The toilet could do with a scrub, but I think we can get Joe or Sophie to do that. Whoever's annoying us most at any given time.'

'We heard that,' Sophie sniped over her shoulder, before turning back to her brother, who had his eyes glued on his phone, his fingers tapping away furiously.

'You were meant to.' Poppy's smile didn't falter. 'It's my not-so-subtle way of telling you not to annoy us. And to avoid that you need to do as you're told, when you're told, and don't walk around with that grimace on your face. You'll scare off the customers.' Ignoring the grunt from Sophie's direction, Poppy focused on Ben. 'So, Ben, have you signed the papers? Does it look good? Are you happy with everything? Do you think we could have this place up and running in a week or two?'

Ben set the papers down, closed his eyes and took a breath. This was too much, too fast. This was pure Poppy. All go, no slow. 'Poppy.' He opened his eyes and took her by the shoulders. 'I'm not sure about this. You and me, running a business in the same room? It's a recipe for disaster.'

'Piffle.' Poppy shook her head, sending her signature black braid swinging. 'We used to make a great team. Aced all the school projects we did together. And sure, we got into a little trouble here and there…'

'Because of you,' Ben asserted, hoping to remind her that her past follies hadn't been forgotten. Even if they had quickly been forgiven.

'Yes, well, I was younger. Now I'm not. Look, I've got the money.' She pulled out her phone and began swiping furiously. 'I have an app that I can show you. I've been saving every penny I can for a couple of years now.' She went to lift her phone, but Ben held up his hand, stopping her.

'It's not that I don't think you have the money. You could get the money in a second, even if you didn't. Your mother, your family, isn't exactly poor…'

Poppy's smile disappeared, the line of her jaw sharpened. Ben inwardly cursed himself. Poppy's mother may have been a successful artist, and the family she came from may have been well off, but that didn't mean Poppy was a pampered princess who was given everything her heart desired. His home had shared a wall with Poppy's, and he'd heard the raised voices when she and her mother had argued, followed by the door slamming.

What had gone on at the Taylor household to cause so much friction, he had no idea; Poppy and her often red-rimmed eyes had refused to speak of it, but he knew enough to know that the relationship she had with her mother wasn't the kind where you asked for money. Or, come to think of it, where you'd turn up on the doorstep after twelve years away expecting your old room back.

And maybe that meant he needed to put his misgivings on pause, to trust Poppy. For all her youthful transgressions she'd come home with a plan, with money to execute that plan, and she'd been the one to find a way to reduce the rent on the space, while hiring two helping hands who she had managed to wrangle into submission with just a few words and the lightest of warnings.

'The thing is, Poppy, what do you know about running a business? It's a big ask to expect me to just leap into this with you. There's a lot of risk involved...'

'And I know how much you hate taking risks, which is why I'm not making you take any. Like I said, I have the money. And while I've never owned a business, I've worked in plenty. I've even been put in charge of a couple. Look, Ben. I'm offering a solution. The rent's lower. We've got two people over there who, despite their surly and disinterested demeanours, I think could actually be quite helpful. More importantly, we've got each other. We can make anything work.' Poppy took his hands in hers and gave them a shake. 'Come on. Trust me. But trust me quick. Look outside.'

Ben twisted round to see a couple hanging around the shop's front window, their noses all but pressed to the glass.

'Monty said it was ours, but if they're willing to pay the full amount…' Poppy let the sentence hang, her eyebrows raised.

Damn it. She was right. And he wanted this place. Had done since he saw the advertisement. The exposed bricks, the polished floorboards, the simple but chic décor. It was perfect for a gourmet tea shop. 'Fine. Pass me the pen.' He took in a deep breath as he scrawled his name, and prayed he wasn't making a mistake.

'Fantastic.' Poppy scooped the papers up from under him. 'Monty. We're all signed up.' She passed the papers to their new landlord then half-danced, half-skipped her way to the front door, opened it and flapped her hands at the would-be tenants. 'Sorry, shop's gone. Good luck with your search. Have a fab day.' She twisted round and rubbed her hands together. 'Right. What are we waiting for? We've got two shops to open. Sophie? Joe? Consider this your last day of freedom. Be here tomorrow morning at nine sharp.' Poppy turned her attention back to Ben. 'As for you and I, let's get the keys and you can take me to my new abode, and we'll nut things out there over a bottle of something yummy. My treat.'

***

'Well, this wasn't what I expected.' Ben did a slow three-sixty as he took in Poppy's new home, tucked away on the top floor of a terraced house that had been converted into flats. The open-plan living and dining area was on the small side, with just enough room for the two-seater couch, coffee table and dining suite. Through an open door he spotted a bed, and another door, which presumably led to the en-suite. Despite its cosiness, it was surprisingly elegant, with white-washed wooden floors throughout, walls painted in a soft grey, and the architraves and skirtings in a fresh white. 'It must be a relief that you were able to rent it furnished.' Ben ran his hand over the cream knotted throw that lay over the soft chestnut-coloured leather couch.

'Yeah, well, I knew I wanted to hit the ground running when I arrived, so it just made sense to find a place that was all set up for me.' Poppy grabbed the bottle of sauvignon blanc she'd picked up on their way home and cracked the lid. 'Screw tops. How did we ever live without them?'

'My father calls them the work of the devil.' Ben rolled his eyes towards the ceiling and shook his head.

Poppy's laughter filled the space, light and free. 'Why does that not surprise me?' She sloshed the wine into two glasses and passed one to Ben. 'So, what made you do such a U-turn? Upping and leaving a safe, secure job in order to start your own business venture? That's not the Ben I grew up with. And, how *is* your father taking it?'

Ben swirled the wine round, creating a miniature maelstrom. He inwardly grimaced; it was the perfect symbol for the current state of his life. 'He's taking it as well as you'd expect. Dad can't get his head around me wanting something other than what he wants for me, if that makes sense. All these years and we've shared the law. Bonded over it. Now… I'm doing what makes me happy. Pursuing a career that fills me with joy in here…' He tapped his heart. 'A career that excites me. I think Dad sees that as a betrayal. Hell, I know he does.' He took a sip of wine, hoping to wash away the grief that had created a knot in his throat. 'We're not really talking right now. Mum's trying to mediate, but…'

'She's wasting her time?' Poppy moved to the small dining table and pushed aside the curtains, allowing the late afternoon light to spill into the room.

'Something like that.' Ben pulled out the chair opposite Poppy, sat down and closed his eyes against the sun, glad for the moment to rest, relax… and try and figure out what the hell he'd just gotten himself into.

'"Why did I agree to this?" That's what you're thinking, isn't it?'

Ben opened his eyes to see the tip of Poppy's tongue peeking out between her lips, a teasing smile lifting her lips.

'I'm not going to screw this up, Ben. I promise. Sparkle & Steep is going to be amazing.' Poppy took a sip of her wine and set the glass down. 'It'll be as brilliant as this view. Look at the view, Ben. Isn't it brilliant?'

Ben turned to the window and saw a length of London sprawling before him, the cityscape rising tall and proud into a bright blue sky. 'You're right, it's brilliant. God, I can't believe you managed to find this place while living on the other side of the world.'

'I'm lucky like that.' Poppy grinned, her fingers rhythmically drumming on the table. 'I'm also lucky to have you. You could have said no to me coming into the shop with you. You could have told me to stay in the car back there. You could have flat out refused to entertain the idea of going into business with me. But you didn't. So, thank you.'

'You're not going to make me regret it, are you?' Ben laid his hand over Poppy's, stopping the incessant drumming.

'No. I'm not. We're going to prove your father wrong. More than that, we're going to make him proud.' Poppy lifted her glass. 'To us. To Sparkle & Steep.'

Ben raised his glass to meet hers, then took a sip as was tradition. Making his father proud. Poppy made it seem so easy. So simple. But how did you make a man proud when you'd walked away from a profession that, for the men in his family, being part of was every bit a tradition as sipping your drink after proposing a toast?

'Stop stewing, Ben.' Poppy sprung up, crossed the room to where she'd dumped her backpack, then unclipped and rifled through it, sending a tattered lump of greyness, with a faded rainbow mane, falling to the floor.

Mr Flumpkins? Surely not? Had Poppy really carried the unicorn she'd found in Alexandra Park and – after being unable to find its owner – decided to adopt, around the world with her? She must've had him for twenty odd years by now.

'Am I seeing things? Is that... Mr Flumpkins?'

Poppy hugged the soft toy to her chest. 'It is. In the cosy, cuddly, fluffy-ish flesh.'

Ben held his hand out, and Poppy passed the toy to him. 'I can't believe he's still in one piece.'

'Barely.' Poppy continued rummaging through her bag. 'He nearly lost his ear in an airport escalator a couple of years back. Fell out of my backpack, nearly got chomped, poor wee soul. Luckily a young girl snatched him up and gave him back before it was too late.'

'I'm surprised she didn't keep him for herself.'

'Hardly. She told me I needed to chuck him and get

myself a newer, prettier one. She liked the ice cream I bought her to say thanks well enough though. Ah, here's what I'm looking for.' She pulled out a shining, shimmering notebook, a pen threaded through its ringed spine. 'We need to plan how we're going to do this thing.'

Ben placed Mr Flumpkins on the windowsill and straightened up. Yes, a plan was needed. Big time. With a plan in place he'd feel less like he'd been shoved into a whirlwind and spat out again.

'So…' Poppy slid into the chair, opened the notebook and wrote the name she'd proposed at the top of a blank page. 'I was thinking we could have multi-coloured chairs scattered around multi-coloured tables. Industrial style metal ones. They'll look amazing. Also, unicorn-headed teaspoons. Oh, and I could get some of those cushions that are covered in sequins that can be brushed two ways to create different patterns so that the chairs are nice and comfy for those who want to sit and natter.' She reached over and grabbed her mobile from its spot on the kitchen bench. 'Find out where to get reversible sequin cushions,' she said aloud as she typed the reminder into her phone. She set the phone down with a satisfied nod. 'I'd sell them as well, of course. They're fabulous.'

Ben blinked, trying to comprehend what he was hearing. So much for being spat out of the whirlwind. What was Poppy on about? Multi-coloured this and that? Sparkly cushions? That wasn't the plan. That wasn't gourmet. It sounded like… a unicorn had eaten too many sweets and thrown up all over the place.

'Nooooo. No. Uh-uh. This won't do. This isn't going to work.' He pushed the chair back, and began to pace the width of the room, trying to get his thoughts in order.

'What do you mean it won't work? It has to. We've signed the lease. We've committed.' Poppy tapped the end of the pen on the notebook. 'I've seen some unicorn-themed clothing that I was planning to sell, but maybe we could find tea lovers' apparel too? Cake lovers' apparel? There must be some out there we could import, or we could create our own?'

Ben's stomach swirled. Tea and cake-loving apparel? Where was the sophistication? The class? This wasn't what he had in mind, not by a long shot. It was like Poppy thought that by sharing a space with him they were joining forces, going into business together. An inseparable team. Just like the old days. But this wasn't the old days. They'd been separated for years now. Gone down different paths. And, if he were one hundred per cent honest with himself, while it was one thing to share a lease, he didn't want to share his shop. Not with someone who could so easily pack up and pick up in the middle of the night without saying a word.

Fear froze his frenetic pacing. And what if she did that anyway? Even if their shops were separate, he'd be left with one surly teen, one disengaged one, and half a shop's worth of lease.

Ben swallowed hard, pushing the lump that was threatening to choke him, to drown his dreams, out of the way. 'Poppy. Ground rules. We need to set some.'

'Ground rules?' Poppy's head angled, her brows drawing together. 'What kind?'

'First of all. You are not to leave in the middle of the night without warning.'

Poppy huffed and rolled her eyes. 'I did it once. Years ago. I'm a grown woman, I'm not going to do that again. I wouldn't do it to you. There's too much riding on this. I get that.'

'Which leads me to the next rule. We have to keep our businesses separate. We can share a space, share the lease, but under no circumstances is any of your... paraphernalia to enter my side of the shop. "Steep" is not to look like a fairy chundered in it. There will be no glitter. No sparkle. No tackiness. No unicorns. My side of the shop—' he placed his hand on his chest to emphasise the point '—is to be a place of refinement. Where people who appreciate good tea will come and discover new flavours and broaden their tea horizons, all while enjoying delicious morsels.'

Poppy rolled her eyes. 'How did you and I ever end up friends? You're such a stick in the mud. And who says "morsels" anymore? Food, Ben. They'll be coming to eat your food.' Poppy placed her hands on her hips. 'Honestly, I can't believe you're so anti-unicorn. I knew

271

I should've set up a cat-themed shop instead. Cat cafes are big business. I went to one in New Zealand and there was something so centring about having a cat purring on your lap while you were sipping a flat white. Although when one decided my braid was a plaything that wasn't so fun. Who knew getting a kitten out of your hair could be so difficult?' Poppy's braid swayed as she shook her head. 'We could do it, you know. Adopt some cats and kittens. A gourmet tea shop with kittens running amuck sounds pretty fab.'

Ben forced himself not to rise to the bait. Poppy had always known how to press his buttons – had been amused by how he toed the line compared to her freedom-loving ways. She, more than anyone, knew he wouldn't have time for the frivolity of kittens and cats skittering through a store, let alone time for cleaning up after them and maintaining their health.

'What? You're not going to tell me I'm being ridiculous?' Poppy laughed, the sound brightening the room, as it had always done. 'I was expecting you to give me that look of derision that I bet had people quailing in court.'

'I wasn't in court, Poppy. You know I worked in property law.' Ben sat back down and took a long drink of his wine.

'Well, you could have been. You could have changed directions, for all I knew. It's not like you've bothered replying to the emails I've sent in the past year or so. Not with any news of substance. "I'm fine" does not an email make.' Poppy crossed her arms and tucked her hands in her armpits.

Guilt swarmed in Ben's gut. That was Poppy's signature move when she was hurt, sad, upset or wanting to shut someone out. And he'd been the cause of it. 'I'm sorry I didn't reply all that much, or all that well. Life got busy. You know how things are. Or maybe you don't... I don't know.'

'Of course you don't know. You didn't ask. Even when we were emailing on a sort-of regular basis you never asked questions about my life.' Poppy sunk her top teeth into her bottom lip, then released them. 'You probably thought my life was one great adventure. Swanning from country to country. Chasing summer. Sunbathing. Swimming. Being frivolous and free while you spent hours poring over papers and whatnot. The thing is, I worked, Ben. The whole time. Yes, I saw sights. Yes, I had a good time. But I also worked my arse off. It wasn't one long holiday.' Poppy's jaw jutted out, just as it always did when she was holding back – trying to keep her emotions in check, trying to be brave. 'Just because I choose to smile instead of scowl, choose to laugh instead of lift my lip and sneer at the world, it doesn't mean I don't have a serious bone in my body. It doesn't mean that I don't *care*.' Poppy untucked her arms, lifted her chin, and took a deep breath in. 'Whatever. It doesn't matter. I'm being an idiot. So, back to business...' She picked up her pen, lowered her gaze to the page so he couldn't see how she was feeling, and scrawled two short sentences.

'*No combining space. No combining anything.*'

Poppy set the pen down on the paper with a slap. And just like that, Ben was a boy again, and the urge to make Poppy feel better was there. The need to reach out and run his hand down her braided rope of ebony hair. To hold her close. To tell her she was wonderful. She was enough. That despite whatever complicated things were happening in her life, in her head, that they could deal with it together. If she just let him in.

Except she wouldn't. He was an idiot to think her time away travelling would have changed that. Changed *her*.

'I know you didn't just sunbathe your way round the world. Sorry. I didn't mean to upset you.'

Poppy waved his apology away. 'I'm fine. Really.' She looked up, a smile fixed on her face. One that didn't chase away the shadows in her eyes. 'If anything, I'm kicking myself. I should have expected this to happen. You've always been so paint-by-numbers. Knowing what you wanted, why you wanted it, and how you were going to get it. You're the most organised person I know. Heck, I bet even your underwear drawer is colour-coded. Light to dark, from left to right. Or is it alphabetised by brand? Or arranged by occasion? Your day-to-day underwear would be at the top, followed by church underwear, because you'd be too respectful to wear anything threadbare or holey to church.'

'I haven't been to church since I moved out of home. I just went because it made Mum happy.'

'But I bet you still go to St James' every Christmas and Easter.' Poppy raised an eyebrow, daring him to deny it.

'I do. With Mum.' Ben nodded, not seeing any point in lying. 'But I don't have special church underwear.'

'But I bet you've got dating underwear. The good stuff. Fits perfectly. Manly colours. Navy blue. Black. No tacky patterns. Although I did see some unicorn boxers that I could order for you if you wanted to shake things up...'

Ben waved Poppy's suggestion away. 'Not in a million years will I wear unicorn boxers. Or unicorn anything. And frankly, Poppy, I'm starting to think you're far too interested in the contents of my underwear.' Ben bit down on his tongue. What had he just said? He surely didn't say 'contents of my underwear'.

He glanced at Poppy who was doubled over, elbows on knees, her shoulders shaking as airy gasps filled the space between them.

'I mean... not my underwear... my contents... er, I mean my drawers. I know you wouldn't be interested in the contents of my...' *Shut up, Ben.* God, what was going on with him? Usually he was calm, collected, in control of what came out of his mouth. But being in the same room as Poppy meant the words flew off his tongue as quickly as they came into his head. It was the Poppy-effect in full flight. Her presence had always left him a little unsteady. Off kilter. Hell, he never put a foot wrong when he was left to his own devices, but whenever she entered his sphere, since the day they met, he'd found himself in all sorts of harmless trouble. Nipping over to his neighbour's house to relieve their tree of apples. Getting tipsy on cider Poppy had stolen from her mother's fridge when they were fifteen. He'd been so ill the next day his parents had taken pity on him and decided the hangover was punishment enough. Life with Poppy was more interesting, but it also meant there was a huge chance things could go askew.

She could promise things were going to go smoothly all she wanted, but he only had the past to go by, and that made him nervous.

'Oh God, you're hilarious. You and your rules.' Poppy straightened up and smoothed back the tendrils of hair that that had come loose from her braid to frame her face. 'You were always one for them, but gosh, look at you now. So serious. So earnest. So much more... rule-y. What happened, Ben? You used to know how to have a bit of fun, but now...' Poppy's gaze started at his perfectly shone shoes, before she worked her way up to his suit pants, his suit jacket, lingered on the tie, then finished on his cut-just-that-day hair. 'Now you're all about looking perfect, and making everything perfect, and *being* perfect.

What's wrong with a little sparkle and shimmer and shine? What's wrong with unicorns? They make people happy. They make people smile. Do you not want to be happy and smiley, Ben?'

Did he not want to be happy? Of course he did. But right now he had too much riding on the success of Steep. If he didn't do well, if leaving his practice had been a mistake, he'd have to deal with the disapproval of his father for... well, probably ever. 'Look, Poppy, I just want to make sure my business succeeds. And for that to happen "Steep" needs to be taken seriously, and unicorns don't exactly project that mentality. It's one thing to go halves in this space, but there needs to be separation. No sharing, no boundary crossing, you understand? "Sparkle" can shimmer and shine all it likes, but "Steep" needs to be as solid and dependable as a good cup of tea.'

Poppy rolled her eyes so hard Ben feared they were going to pop out of their sockets. 'Fine. I understand. I'll stick to your stupid rule, but I've got one rule you need to abide by.'

'Really?' Ben mashed his lips together to stop a smirk appearing. Poppy, the ultimate disregarder of rules, was going to set one? 'What's your rule?'

'My rule is this – if you so much as look at one of my customers like they're mad for loving unicorns, if you so much as make a snide remark, if I see a hint of side-eye when a man comes in and buys the unicorn underpants I plan on selling, then I'm out. I'll give you plenty of time to find a person to take over my side of the space. Or enough time for you to see your bank manager, or whoever, and sort out your expanding into my side of the shop, but I won't stick around. You take 'Steep' seriously? Well, I take 'Sparkle' every bit as seriously. My life savings are going into this, and I don't have assets I can sell or people I can ask to help me should things falter. Which, they won't.'

Ben nodded. 'You're right, they won't. Because as much as I'm sure I could fill the space or figure out some alternative arrangement, I have neither the time nor the inclination. So, I guess that means I agree to your ridiculous rule.'

'Good.' Poppy held out her hand for Ben to shake and caught the edge of her wine glass, knocking it over, which saw it domino into his wine glass, sending a stream of wine over the table and onto the floor.

Please don't be a sign. Ben shook his head in despair. *Please don't let it mean that 'Sparkle & Steep' is destined to become 'Debacle & Weep'.*